He'd been waiting f...
Isabella Roman...

He'd dated now and ... kept it casual. But now...

And he wanted it with ... ...

Her family just happened to be a bonus.

"Ethan." Mandy interrupted his thoughts. He glanced over at her. "When I say Isa's a challenge, I mean it. If you want to win her heart, you'll have to dive in for the long haul."

Just then Isa joined them, breathless with laughter.

"What were you two talking about?" Isa whispered to Ethan.

He shrugged. "You."

She smiled as though she didn't mind.

"I want to remind you that you *did* say you were looking for more chaos in your life, remember?" Isa teased.

Ethan winked at her, leaning closer until Isa held her breath.

"I'm pretty sure I found the chaos I was looking for, Isabella." He whispered the words so only she could hear them.

"Did you just associate me with pandemonium, Ethan Carter?" she whispered back.

"You said it, Isabella Romano," Ethan answered with a grin.

INSPIRATIONAL
FICTION

Books by Brandy Bruce

Love Inspired Heartsong Presents

Table for Two
Second Chance Café

BRANDY BRUCE

has worked in book publishing for nine years—editing, writing, reading and making good use of online dictionaries. She's a graduate of Liberty University, and currently works as a part-time nonfiction book editor. She and her husband, Jeff, make their home in Colorado with their two children, Ashtyn and Lincoln. Brandy loves reading, writing, watching movies based on Jane Austen books, baking cheesecake and spending time with her family.

BRANDY BRUCE

Second Chance Café

HEARTSONG
PRESENTS

Recycling programs for this product may not exist in your area.

LOVE INSPIRED BOOKS

ISBN-13: 978-0-373-48719-6

SECOND CHANCE CAFÉ

Copyright © 2014 by Brandy Bruce

www.Harlequin.com

Printed in U.S.A.

I am come that they might have life,
and that they might have it more abundantly.
—*John* 10:10

For my mom and dad.
You've both always given me so much love;
my cup runs over.

Acknowledgments

Mike Brock and my sister Sara Hanson with FinishLine
Physical Therapy in Highlands Ranch, CO, thank
you both *so* much for all your amazing help with this
book. Mike, thanks for explaining things like nerve
entrapment to me! Shirlee Davis, Sherilyn Smith,
and Stephanie McHenry, thank you for sharing
your expertise as nurses with me. I could not have
finished this book without all of you! Any mistakes are
entirely mine. And a special thank you to my mother,
Blanca Brumble, who flew to Colorado to help
in so many ways so I would have time to write.
And as always, thanks to my husband, Jeff, for watching
the kids while I work, for brainstorming ideas with me,
and for encouraging me.

Chapter 1

"Okay, people. We've got a firefighter with possible fractures and trauma to the spine. ETA is five minutes."

Nurse Isabella Romano's ears perked up and her pulse quickened. The mood in the emergency room shifted to one of controlled urgency. Isabella slipped on gloves and followed the attending physician, Dr. Nichols, to the Denver Health Medical Center's E.R. entrance. Sirens rang out in the distance, and within minutes the familiar sight of flashing lights sped toward them.

The back doors of the ambulance flew open and the paramedics jumped out. "Male, late twenties, fell from second-story landing to first floor and landed on his back. Multiple burns on his arms and a laceration on his right thigh. Hypotensive. Tachycardic. We administered 1 liter of saline through an 18-gauge IV in his left AC. Patient has maintained a pulse ox of 96 percent on 10 liters of oxygen via face mask."

Isabella grabbed the left side of the stretcher, helping push the gurney to trauma room 1. At the sound of a low moan, she looked down at the firefighter strapped to the backboard. A neck collar kept him immobile and an oxygen mask covered his mouth and nose.

"What's his name?" Isabella called out to the EMT across from her.

"Ethan Carter. Company 51. Those guys will be filling up the waiting room as soon as they clear the scene."

She bent over him. "Ethan, I'm Isabella. Can you hear me?"

His gaze met hers and Isabella could see his intense pain.

"Ethan, you're going to be okay. We're going to take good care of you."

"Okay, everyone, on three," Dr. Nichols ordered.

Everyone stopped what they were doing at the doctor's instruction and lifted the backboard with Ethan on it, transferring him and the backboard to the hospital bed. He moaned. "We're going to need 50 mcg of fentanyl," Dr. Nichols called out. Maggie, one of Isabella's colleagues, began cutting off Ethan's burned clothing.

"Let's get some X-rays, Isa," Dr. Nichols stated. "I want a CT scan. His thigh obviously needs stitches."

"I'm on it," Maggie said as she inspected the burns on Ethan's arms. Isabella moved to order the X-rays but Ethan reached out for her. She stepped back toward him, preparing to explain to him that she'd be back and he was going to be all right. But the look in his blue eyes stopped her. He tried to reach for his oxygen mask, but Isabella shook her head.

"No, don't move," she said, then pulled away his mask for a moment.

"Don't leave me," he said, his voice dry and raspy. Isabella was pretty sure that even covered in dust and blood, with a brace around his neck, he was the most attractive man she'd ever seen. Her heart tugged. In that moment, he just seemed so alone.

She replaced his oxygen. "I have to go for a minute, Ethan, but I'll be coming right back. And we'll get through this together. I know you're scared and I know you're hurting. But it's going to be okay."

He just stared at her, his eyes pleading for her to stay. Isabella couldn't help it; she reached down and brushed his brown hair from his forehead.

"I promise I'll be back," she told him.

Ethan Carter's eyes fluttered open and then shut again quickly.

Who in the world turned on that blinding light?

He could hear a voice, someone saying his name. He turned his head to the side.

What happened?

He heard that voice again, saying his name. Then it came back to him, playing through his mind like a movie reel. The house fire. The roaring sound of the blaze. The sensation that he was falling. The impact of the ground floor. The rush into the E.R.

"Ethan?"

He opened his eyes and blinked, trying to focus on the woman's face in front of him.

"Hi there," she said. "It's nice to see you again."

He blinked again. "Nurse..."

"Isabella. We met under rather tragic circumstances, I know."

She was teasing. He could hear it in her voice. Now that he could focus on her clearly, he remembered seeing her in the E.R.

"Isabella," he repeated. Dressed in blue scrubs, she stood next to the bed, her brown hair tied back in a knot. She smiled down at him and Ethan felt better at the sight of her smile. She checked the monitors, her eyes darting toward the door of the hospital room.

"Did they get the family out of the house?" Ethan asked. Isabella nodded.

"Yes. One of the other firefighters—I think his name was Blake—told me to let you know that everyone made it out safely."

"Except me, I guess," Ethan said grimly. But Isabella's smile didn't fade.

"C'mon, tough guy. You've got this."

Ethan studied her warm smile and playful tone. "You're right," he conceded. "God was watching over me in that burning house. He won't abandon me now."

She blinked in surprise at his statement. "I suppose He was," she agreed.

"When can I go home?" Ethan asked.

"I'm not sure," Isabella answered. "Dr. Nichols will be here any minute to talk to you," she said.

"Can you stay?" Ethan asked. Her face softened.

"Sure, if you want me to. Is there anyone you want me to call for you? The guys from the firehouse were here all night, off and on, in the waiting room. There are a few guys out there now. They can come in as soon as Dr. Nichols speaks to you."

Ethan nodded. "Thanks. But there's no one else for you to call."

Isabella frowned. "Your family?"

Ethan just shook his head, turning his attention to the gauze covering his forearms. "There's no one. Just the guys." He hoped she'd drop the topic. He hated the pitiful looks he got whenever he explained to people that other than a few distant relatives out in California, he had no one. It was part of why he'd joined Company 51. A whole firehouse with the brothers he'd never had. He wondered if the chief was in the waiting room.

The door slid open and a doctor wearing black-rimmed glasses and holding a clipboard walked in. He looked to be in his mid-forties.

"Good morning, Ethan. How are we feeling today?"

We? I have a feeling you're doing a lot better than I am, Doc.

"I'm hurting, but I'm guessing that medication is dulling the real pain."

Dr. Nichols nodded. "You had a bad fall, Ethan. You know that. There were second-degree burns on your arms and a gash on your thigh that took about twenty stitches. You lost some blood, but we've given you IV fluids and your vitals have stabilized. You're pretty banged up and bruised all over, but unfortunately, your back took the impact of the fall."

Ethan's chest constricted with fear.

"How bad is it?"

Isabella stepped closer to his bedside.

"It could have been worse. You have a lumbar—lower back—spinal fracture. The X-ray showed an L4 compression fracture. The positive aspect of this is that you still have good movement and feeling. Also, there doesn't seem to be any neurological damage."

"Do I need surgery?" Ethan asked.

"I don't think so. The X-rays indicate a clean fracture. I'm going to recommend we move forward with outpatient treatment. But you've got a long, arduous healing journey ahead of you."

"How long until I can be back on active duty?"

Dr. Nichol's eyebrows furrowed. "The spine is a tricky

thing, Ethan. And everyone heals at a different pace. You're going to need rest, pain medication, lots of therapy, a back brace—"

"How long?" Ethan insisted.

"We're talking months. And that's assuming that everything heals as it should. While in a few weeks you'll be able to continue with most day-to-day activities, I don't see you going back to active duty for probably six months. It could be less. It could be more. Perhaps they can transfer you to a desk job until you're ready. After a few weeks of therapy we could reevaluate and consider light duty. But as of right now, your life is going to look different. You need to understand and accept that. Your priority needs to be healing properly."

Months? Desk job? Light duty? Ethan tried to swallow the boulder in his throat.

"But eventually, I'll be back to normal. I'll be able to be on active duty, right?" Ethan pressed. Dr. Nichols folded his arms across his clipboard.

"If all goes as it should, I think you'll make a full recovery. But as I said, this is going to be a one-day-at-a-time healing process. We'll start with rest. I want you on complete bed rest for the next few days. No strenuous activity. We'll fit you for a back brace, which I want you to wear for six to eight weeks. We'll do an X-ray after six weeks and see if the bone has healed. Then, once the bone has healed, you'll need to begin physical therapy."

Ethan took a deep breath. He felt a soft hand squeeze his arm and he looked up at Isabella.

"Hey, it's going to be okay," she said, her voice encouraging. "You're here, you're alive, you're going to be able to walk—those are all good things." He stared at her, trying to hold on to the sense of calm emanating from her.

She's right, Father, he prayed. *But what am I going to*

do for months if I'm not fighting fires? And what if "the healing process" doesn't go as it should and I can't go back? Company 51 is all I have.

That last thought was too much. Ethan felt tears welling up in his eyes. He blinked fast to keep them at bay, mortified that he might cry in front of this nurse who not only was kind and smart and had a great sense of humor but also looked stunning in blue scrubs.

I will never leave you.

The words were just a whisper in his heart, but they were enough. He clung to them. It had been only six months since one of his brothers at the firehouse, Caleb, had led Ethan to Christ. Six months of a changed life. He still struggled to accept that God loved him like a father. That he could turn to God at any time. But it was getting easier. Accepting Christ as his Savior had filled Ethan with something he'd known was missing since childhood. Now he treasured that faith more than anything else.

Ethan closed his eyes.

I have You, Father. Whatever comes, I have you. Help me through this.

Isabella watched as Ethan closed his eyes. His lips moved silently, and she knew without a doubt that he was praying. She looked over at Dr. Nichols, who stood waiting. Prayers were common things in the hospital. Sometimes people cried out loudly for help. Sometimes it was a desperate whisper. And sometimes, like now, it was a silent request. She'd seen people blame God. She'd seen them beg for His comfort. She'd even seen them try to barter for what they wanted.

Isabella wondered which one Ethan was doing now.

She also considered the fact that without all the dust and

blood, Ethan Carter was even more attractive than she'd found him to be in the E.R.

He had no family to call. That's odd. The firefighters have filled up the waiting room, of course. But no one else. No relatives. No girlfriend. No one.

Isabella stared at the handsome firefighter's brown hair and dark brown eyebrows. His sturdy jaw and those lips. She watched him pray. She wasn't sure if it was appropriate to think so or not, but the fact that he was praying made him even more attractive.

I was wrong. He's not completely alone. He has faith.

Ethan drew a breath and opened his eyes. He looked at Isabella before turning his attention to Dr. Nichols.

"Okay, what's my next step, Doc?"

Chapter 2

"Flowers again, Isa?" Maggie said in mock surprise before leaning over and breathing in the scent from the large bouquet of white roses sitting on the counter of the E.R. administration desk. Isabella rolled her eyes. The two had been working the night shift in the E.R. together for six months. At thirty-two years old, Maggie was five years older than Isabella but the two were fast friends. Maggie leaned back and rubbed her bulging five-and-half-months-pregnant belly. Out of habit, Isabella's gaze searched Maggie's face for signs of exhaustion. Most of the staff were aware that Maggie had suffered two miscarriages in the past, and making sure this pregnancy went safely and smoothly was a high priority for everyone in the E.R., Isabella most of all. After assuring herself that Maggie looked fine, Isabella waved off Maggie's comment.

"You're jealous."

"You know I am. I can't remember the last time José sent me flowers."

"I can. He sent daisies on your birthday, Maggie."

"This is the second time that good-looking fireman has sent you flowers in the past two weeks. Am I right?"

"Who's counting?"

"Everybody. How does he have these things delivered in the middle of the night?" Maggie asked.

"He gets his firefighter buddies to bring them."

"Adorable." Maggie grinned.

"So he's grateful, Maggie. So what?" Isabella's eyes scanned the computer screen in front of her.

"How can you be so indifferent? How many times has he asked you out now?"

Isabella sighed loudly so Maggie couldn't possibly miss her exasperation.

"How many times has Mr. Matthews proposed to you in the last hour?"

Maggie groaned. "That doesn't count. He's eighty-six. And I'm already married, thank you."

"I've got bad luck when it comes to relationships, Maggie."

"In the past that was true. But this guy could be the one."

"I'm on a dating break."

"Good grief. You choose to take that break the minute a gorgeous fireman walks into your life?"

"Technically, he was wheeled into my life."

With a huff, Maggie grabbed her stack of clipboards and left to check on patients.

Isabella leaned back in her chair, rubbed her shoulders and stared at the roses. They *were* beautiful. Just like the last batch of spring flowers he'd sent. And the card had read the same: "Isabella, I'm still waiting. Ethan."

Isabella smiled at the thought. She liked Ethan's persistence, if truth be told. But after a string of failed relationships and two disastrous attempts at online dating, she had no intention of diving into another disappointment.

Before he'd even been discharged, Ethan had asked her for her phone number, which she'd declined to give him—though she hadn't been *entirely* against it. There were rules against nurses fraternizing with patients, even firemen with gorgeous blue eyes. She'd encouraged him to concentrate on his recovery. A few days after being discharged, he'd requested her friendship via online social networking, which rather impressed Isabella. The guy wouldn't give up. Isabella felt comfortable extending at least electronic friendship to him. So they'd chatted regularly over the past couple of weeks while Ethan endured bed rest and limited mobility. Isabella had grown to enjoy their witty banter online, but a real date?

She looked back at the flowers.

Maybe.

As the sun rose, Isabella's shift ended. With a yawn, she slung her purse over her shoulder and walked out to her car, enjoying the sunrise and balancing her bouquet of flowers in her arms. Summer had come early to Colorado, and Isabella couldn't have been happier about it. She loved the warm sunshine.

Isabella stopped in her tracks at the sight of Ethan Carter standing stiffly by her car.

"What are you doing here?" she said, then inwardly reminded herself to be nice. He *had* just sent her flowers, after all. At the sight of his hopeful smile, she eased up even more.

"I'm wondering if I can take you to breakfast."

Isabella squinted up at Ethan. The guy must have been six-three, and at just five-four Isabella felt tiny next to him.

"How's your back feeling?" she asked.

He looked at her with those cool blue eyes that she found just a little unnerving. "It hurts."

She knew he wasn't asking for pity, and she appreciated his honesty.

"Come on, Isabella. It's only breakfast. You saved my life. I owe you that."

Isabella was already putting her keys back into her pocket. "I didn't save your life, Ethan."

"You helped," he insisted.

"I already have plans. Sorry," she said, waiting to see if he'd take the bait.

"You already have plans? Really? Cancel. What I'm offering can't be beat."

Curiosity got the better of her. "What are you offering?" she asked.

"Monday mornings they serve pancakes at the fire station."

"Hmm." She looked down at her flowers. "What about these?"

"Leave them here. Let the staff enjoy them all day."

"Okay. Wait for me," Isabella said as she turned back toward the E.R. entrance.

"That's all I seem to do lately!" Ethan called out after her. Isabella grinned from ear to ear.

Twenty minutes later Ethan sat across from Isabella Romano, relieved beyond belief that she'd actually said yes to breakfast with him. They sat at the end of the long dining table at the fire station. He drenched his short stack in syrup and listened to the guys pepper Isabella with questions. He had a feeling she could hold her own with the rowdy crew of Company 51.

The guys had been thrilled to have him stop by. He'd known they would be. The men who made up Company

51 had been his support system, taking him to doctors' appointments during those first weeks when he couldn't drive. A few of the firefighters' wives had brought over meals. He missed the camaraderie even more than he missed the work. But as he sat with difficulty in the folding chair, he couldn't ignore the ache in his back. The doctor hadn't been kidding when he'd said it was a bad fall. Ethan hated feeling so confined by his injury. The medication didn't seem to be enough to eradicate the pain.

"Ethan?" His attention jolted at the sound of Isabella's voice. "Are you okay?"

He paused for a moment, distracted by her. Her curly shoulder-length dark hair framed her face. Her chocolate-brown eyes focused on Ethan in a way that made him struggle to speak. And even though she was obviously tired, she seemed completely present and glad to be with him.

"I need to get back to work. Staying home makes me crazy," he told her.

"You know it will be a while," she responded.

Ethan stabbed a forkful of pancakes and didn't answer.

"Did you always want to be a nurse?" he asked, ready for a change of subject.

Isabella didn't seem to mind. "Well, since college. I didn't really want to go into the family business, and medicine had always intrigued me."

"Family business?" Ethan echoed.

Isabella sipped her orange juice. "My father owned a big restaurant in Los Angeles when I was a little girl. He moved our family to Denver when I was in middle school—we had extended family living here—and he opened a second restaurant. They were both very successful. A couple of years ago he and my brother opened a third restaurant in downtown Denver. It's a little bit of a departure from the first two restaurants, but it's done well. Sadly, my father suffers from Parkinson's. So he sold the Los Angeles restaurant to my uncle, and my older brother took over both Denver restaurants."

"Wow! I'm taking a wild guess that you're talking about the Romano's restaurants."

Isabella swirled a forkful of pancakes through the maze of syrup on her plate. "The very ones."

Ethan took note of her measured response and filed that away for a later discussion. "That's amazing, Isabella. I've always wondered what it would be like to own a restaurant."

"It's a lot of hard work. Restaurant life is all-encompassing. Exhausting. Stressful." Her tone said it all.

"But that's true of most jobs," Ethan countered. "I would imagine nursing is exhausting and stressful."

Isabella looked thoughtful. "You're right. I guess it's just a question of whether it's the kind of exhausting, stressful work you find invigorating and satisfying, versus just a job that wears you out and leaves you frustrated."

"So you don't like cooking?" Ethan clarified.

"No, I love cooking. I do. That seems to run in the blood of my family. I grew up in the kitchen, cooking with my mom and dad and Leo, my brother. And I worked in my father's restaurants all through high school and college. Food is very important to my family. While I'm not crazy about restaurant life, I love food."

"Me too. I used to do most of the cooking here at the station whenever I was on shift."

"Really?" Isabella sounded surprised. "So what's your specialty?"

Ethan shrugged. "Whatever we've got in the kitchen. I can make a mean grilled tomato, chicken and cheese sandwich."

"Sounds good. Would you make one for me sometime?" Isabella asked.

He winked at her. "Name the time and place, Isabella Romano, and you've got yourself a date."

She chuckled. "Good to know. I'll get back to you on that."

Ethan liked Isabella's tendency to joke easily and take things in stride. But he wanted her to feel that she could share even more serious topics with him.

He lowered his tone to avoid all of Company 51 hearing. "I'm sorry to hear that your father has Parkinson's. That must be difficult."

Isabella looked down at the table. "It is. He's always been so strong and able. It's hard to watch him grow weak and frail. But he's a man of faith."

Ethan's eyes lit up. "He's a believer?"

"Yes. I am, too. Most of my family members are believers. What about you?"

"About six months ago my friend Caleb introduced me to Jesus. My life has changed."

Isabella finished the last bite of her pancake and then glanced at her watch. "Wow, is it nine already? I need to get back, Ethan. I've got to get some sleep and then I have errands to run before my shift tonight."

Ethan sat quietly, watching her for a moment.

It's like she shut down right as we began talking about faith.

He wiped his mouth and grabbed his keys. "Of course. I'll take you back to your car at the hospital." After a round of goodbyes from the firefighters, Ethan and Isabella made their way to his truck.

The drive back to the hospital was filled with mostly light chitchat, though Ethan wished he could ask more about her family and her faith. He wanted to know everything about her, but Isabella seemed so guarded. He didn't want to push too hard. She was the same way whenever they chatted online—she kept the conversation light and funny and short, rarely willing to go into deeper topics.

"Thanks for breakfast, Ethan. I had a really good time."

"Does that mean you're open to having dinner with me? Or should I push for lunch next?"

Isabella laughed and the sound warmed Ethan all over.

"I'd say lunch. Don't press your luck."

That afternoon, while wearing his back brace and feeling bored to tears, Ethan sat at the coffee bar at O'Brien's, the small café next door to the fire station. He kept thinking over Isabella's description of restaurant life. All-encompassing, exhausting, stressful—the same could be said about fighting fires, yet he thrived on it.

There was no way that Isabella could know he'd harbored a secret dream of opening his own restaurant one day. The dream had started back in college when he'd worked at a diner for extra money. After he'd had a quick run as a busboy, they'd trained him to be a short-order cook out of sheer desperation. One of the cooks had quit and they'd needed help. While it was supposed to be only temporary, he'd loved being in the kitchen and had ended up working there until he'd finished school. Other than being a firefighter, it was the only thing that had ever really interested him. He'd even taken a few cooking classes at The Seasoned Chef in Denver.

"Ethan, haven't seen you in a while."

Ethan looked up as Mick O'Brien, the owner of the café, climbed up on a barstool next to him, groaning as he plopped into his seat. It was common knowledge that Mick had a soft spot in his heart for the guys at the firehouse. His own son was a paramedic in Fort Collins. More than once

Ethan had joked with Mick about taking over O'Brien's so Mick could travel the world with his wife, Kay.

"How's the back injury?" Mick asked.

"I suppose it's going to take some time," Ethan admitted.

Mick nodded. "But you think you'll be able to go back to work?"

"That's what they tell me," Ethan said with determination.

"I see." Mick called out to Annie, one of the waitresses, for a cup of coffee. She took her time bringing it over. Ethan thought, not for the first time, that the service at O'Brien's left something to be desired.

"How are things going for you, Mick?" Ethan asked, taking note that he was one of only five customers and it was lunchtime.

Mick shook his head. "Days have been better. I need to sell this place, Ethan. You know that. I know that. Kay wants me to sell up and take her to Alaska. She's been bit by a travel bug."

Ethan chuckled. "What about you? Have you been bit by the retirement bug?"

"Bit? Try swallowed up. I've been ready to retire for years. We had a few good years here, but times have changed. I'm not even breaking even. If I can't sell this place, I'm afraid it's going to ruin my retirement plans."

Ethan nodded soberly. "Why not breathe some new life into this old café? Hire new people, change up the menu, redecorate… Maybe that would help."

Mick peered at him with interest. "That's exactly what it needs, Ethan. New life. And you're the one to do it. If I invest any more money into this place, I won't be able to take Kay to Alaska."

Ethan shook his head. "I couldn't take on a business like this, Mick. Look at me. I'm wearing a back brace."

"You won't be for long. I think you could make something special of this restaurant, Ethan. And what are you doing right now, anyway? You can't go back to fighting fires at the moment. You can sit around and wait for your back to heal, or you could take on a new venture while you wait. It might work, Ethan. You might make this café a success again."

He'd heard the words before, but for some reason, this time they sunk into Ethan and the notion took root.

"I doubt I could get a loan," Ethan said, though he wasn't sure. He didn't make all that much as a firefighter, but he was pretty good with investments and had a healthy savings.

"I'll sell it for a fair price, Ethan. I'd rather you have this place than anyone else."

Ethan felt a catch in his throat. Over the years, Mick and Kay had sort of adopted the guys at the fire station. Kay brought over cookies and sandwiches every now and then. And Mick always took time to sit and talk with the fire-fighters who came into the café. And Ethan, who had almost no family to speak of, didn't take those things lightly. He cared about Mick and Kay.

"You take some time to pray about it, Ethan," Mick said after a moment. "And Kay and I will pray about it, too. Call me in a few days if you're interested and I'll have a price for you. I've got a feeling this is right, but you've got to feel it, too."

Someone in the back called for Mick and he lowered himself from the barstool, patting Ethan on the shoulder as he passed by. Alone with his thoughts, Ethan let himself consider the idea of owning his own café. He gazed around the small restaurant.

It needed fresh paint; that was for sure. And new decor. The menu could use some sprucing up, too. A more energized waitstaff wouldn't hurt, either. But the bones of the old place were good. And the location alone gave the café potential. Mick had only ever served breakfast and lunch. Ethan would want to continue that system.

I could still work evenings at the firehouse once I'm cleared for duty.

A new name…new management… Ethan wondered if maybe he really could breathe life into this little place. He could make it his own. Owning a restaurant was a dream he'd given up.

Maybe it was time to take it back.

Chapter 3

The kitchen at the Franklin Street Romano's location buzzed with activity. Isabella walked through the back door, sidestepping waiters, dishwashers and cooks. The smells of marinara, Alfredo sauce and garlic inundated her senses as she quickly navigated through the kitchen maze to make her way to her brother's office. She tapped three times on the door before opening it.

"Leo?"

Her brother looked up in surprise. "Hey, sis. Are you on the schedule for tonight?" he joked. She sat down in the chair across from his desk.

"Very funny."

"So what's up?"

"How's Mandy?" Isabella asked, wondering about her very pregnant sister-in-law and hoping to put off the questions about why she'd dropped by.

"She's okay. Uncomfortable, but it won't be for much longer."

"Two more weeks, right?"

"Yeah. She thinks the baby will come early."

"It's her first. He will probably come late."

"That's what I keep telling her."

"She's a pregnant woman, Leonardo. Don't argue with her right now."

Leo grinned. "*Now* you tell me."

Isabella picked at a stray string on the chair she was sitting in and didn't say anything.

"Like I said, Isa, *what's up?* You never stop by unless you want me to feed you or you need to talk."

Isabella glanced up sheepishly. "I know."

"So which is it?"

"Both. Can I get an order of spinach lasagna to take with me?"

"You know you can. Now tell me what's going on with you."

Isabella sighed. "I had breakfast with a firefighter today."

Leo's eyebrows rose. "So, you've come to me with your boy problems?"

"Leonardo," Isabella warned, and Leo held up both hands.

"Sorry, sorry. I'm all ears. When can I meet him?"

"I don't know. It's not serious or anything. It was the first time we've hung out together in person. We chat online sometimes."

"But you like him," Leo said after a moment, studying her. "Why?"

Isabella crossed her arms. "I don't know. He just had a really bad back injury and yet he still tries to stay positive. He's persistent, which I like. I can't stand measly guys who won't go after what they want. But he's not forceful. He's laid-back, but he's capable. And he likes me, which I like."

"And which tells me he has good taste."

Isabella gave her brother a grateful look.

"He's a Christian," she finally said. Leo nodded, then stood up and moved to sit in the chair next to her.

"That's a good thing," he said.

"I know," Isabella agreed.

After a moment of silence—Leo knew her well enough to know not to press her—Isabella laid her head back in the chair.

"Do you ever feel like you've been going through the motions for so long that you don't know what's real anymore?"

A knock at the door interrupted them. Their cousin Angelina poked her head in the office. "Leo, did you want to see me?"

"I did, but it has to wait, Angie. Talk to me after your shift."

"Got it. See you later, Isa." The door closed and Leo looked back at her.

"Have you seen Dad today?" he asked.

Isabella nodded. "Of course. I stopped by right before I came here."

Leo didn't say anything, but she knew what he was thinking. That her lack of faith had to do with their father's debilitating illness.

"You don't have to go over there every day, Isa. They have a trained nurse."

"I'm a trained nurse."

"I know you are," Leo said. "And you're an amazing nurse. But I think going over to Mom and Dad's so much is starting to drain you."

"I want to go. If something happens, it's important to me to be there for him."

"I can understand that because I feel the same way. But you need to have time for a life, too."

"Hello? Did you hear me tell you I went on a date this morning?"

Leo smiled at her propensity to be sassy.

"I'm tired, I guess," Isabella admitted. "I'm feeling a little burned out at the hospital. And yes, going to Mom and Dad's every day wears me out. And even though I want to find someone, I'm really sick of dating. Remember that last guy I dated? The teacher who had a checklist for his future wife that he brought with him to our dinner date? And how awkward it was when he realized I only met two of his checkpoints?"

Leo laughed but started coughing when Isabella gave him the *look*.

"Right. I remember that. Very unfortunate."

"I'm twenty-seven years old and I've never been in a relationship that lasted longer than six months. They just never work out. I get restless or the guy gets restless, or there's not enough chemistry or...I don't know. And I'm just tired of looking. You know, putting myself out there in the dating pool. Risking my heart. I'm not into it anymore."

"You're going to find someone, Isa. It'll happen. You want to stop looking? Go ahead and stop. Hand it over to God and wait and see what happens. But the restlessness in you—I think it's more than just being single."

Isabella stood up and began to pace—nervous habit. When she realized she was doing it, she sat back down and hugged her arms around herself. "I've been going to the same church for what feels like forever. Well, I *used* to be going to the same church. I'm not going to pretend I've been there in months. I just feel like nothing changes for me. I'm always talking to the same people. I've been working as a nurse for years, doing the same job every day. I'm tired of my apartment. I'm tired of watching my dad's health deteriorate and not being able to do anything about it. I'm tired of everything."

Leo rubbed his chin. "So you need a change."

"Yes, Einstein. Any suggestions?"

"Vacation?"

"I'm not comfortable leaving Dad right now. You know he's getting worse."

"I have an opening for a hostess position."

"Leo, don't even go there."

"I was just offering! I'm trying to help. Maybe you should give this firefighter guy a chance. Go out with him. But let me meet him so I can intimidate him."

"He goes into burning buildings for a living. Sorry, bro. I don't think you'll scare him."

"Just think about it."

Isabella sighed. "Okay. My life could use some spicing up."

Leo reached over and touched her hand. "Give God a chance, too, Isa."

She closed her eyes for a moment. "You know I'm a believer, Leo."

"I know you are. But I also know you're not feeling it right now."

"Sometimes I wish God would just do something drastic in my life so that I would know it was really Him. So that I would feel like He's really and truly involved. Like He cares."

"I used to feel that way, too," Leo said. Isabella looked at him, surprised by his admission.

"What happened?"

"When I started looking for Him, I could see His involvement in every way—drastic or not. He's there, Isa."

For the next week and a half, Ethan thought and prayed over the idea of buying the café. He just wasn't sure what to do. He'd chatted online with Isa every few nights but hadn't felt able to broach the subject with her. He kept thinking of her tone and body language when she'd talked to him about her family's restaurant endeavors. He also hadn't had any luck securing another date with her, which troubled him.

It was time to make something happen. He decided to spend some time in the kitchen. Cooking and baking—his ideas of therapy. The kitchen in his studio apartment was small but functional, and Ethan had supplied it with excellent cooking equipment.

It had been months since his last cooking class at The Seasoned Chef. At the time, a guest instructor from France had surprised the class by teaching them to make an assortment of pastries. Ethan had liked *pain au chocolat,* chocolate-stuffed croissants, best. They were a perfect breakfast pastry in Ethan's opinion.

He wondered whether Isabella liked chocolate for breakfast.

The question begged to be answered. Ethan rolled up his sleeves, deciding to dive into the laborious task of making a pastry that would impress Isabella Romano.

He checked his pantry to make sure he had the ingredients for croissants and then got to work mixing flour, sugar, yeast and salt. He poured milk into his stand mixer and added the flour combination, creating a large ball of dough. He ate leftover pizza and watched two movies while waiting for the dough to suitably chill. Folding the dough and making sure it was adequately buttered was time-consuming. About halfway through the ordeal, Ethan had to stop to take his pain medication. He glanced at the clock above his stove, shocked that half the night had passed as he worked. But he didn't mind. The feeling of rolling dough and the sight of scattered ingredients filling his kitchen counters energized him.

By the time the kitchen smelled of a blend of chocolate and warm, fresh croissant bread, Ethan sat at the kitchen table exhausted. He downed an energy drink, trying to stay awake, and then tasted the result of his efforts.

Ethan bit into the warm, flaky bread and was instantly lost in buttery layers, that is, until he stumbled upon the burst of deep melted chocolate.

It was better than he'd expected. He packaged several and left for the hospital, determined to make it there before Isabella's shift ended.

Isabella checked the clock again. Five forty-eight Thursday morning. She yawned. The E.R. had been slower than usual. Slow nights were the hardest. She didn't feel so tired when working amid the rush of a busy emergency room. Maggie had the night off, which made for an even quieter night for Isabella. She sifted through the paperwork in front of her.

I'm exhausted. I don't want to be here right now.

She resisted the urge to glance back up at the clock.

"Isabella, you have a guest." Isabella jerked her head up at Dr. Nichol's statement. He winked at her. "The break room is free, if you want to offer him some coffee." Isabella leaned to the side to see who was standing a few paces behind the doctor.

Someone with the makings of a firefighter.

She bit back her smile. Dr. Nichols walked away and Isabella sat back in her chair.

"Up a little early, aren't you?" she asked.

He walked up to the desk and held out a paper bag. "Breakfast."

Isabella accepted the bag and peered inside, inhaling the aroma of warm bread and chocolate.

"Where did you stop?"

"This is from the kitchen of Ethan Carter."

Isabella looked up with delight. "Well, then. I can offer you some not-that-great coffee, if you're interested."

"If it's coffee with you, Isabella, I'm interested."

Isabella stared at him for a moment, enjoying the quickening of her heart rate at Ethan's words. She liked his self-confidence.

He's good.

"Come on, tough guy," she said, motioning for him to follow her down the hallway. They entered the staff break room and Ethan sat down at the table while Isabella filled two foam cups with lukewarm coffee. She sat next to him and he pointed to the bag of pastry.

"Eat," he insisted. She chuckled and pulled out the still-warm croissant.

"I should warn you, I'll be completely honest with my assessment."

Ethan nodded. "I'd expect nothing less from an expert like you."

Isabella bit into the croissant and paused, appreciating the light, flaky texture and rich, buttery taste. The chocolate was obviously high quality, rich and delicious.

"Mmm." The response was unplanned but completely accurate. Ethan's smile reached his eyes.

"I assume that means you approve?"

Isabella took another bite before answering.

"So…why didn't you tell me?"

"Tell you what?"

"That you lead a secret double life as a pastry chef?"

Ethan laughed. "Don't tell the guys at the fire station, okay?"

Isabella watched him, wishing for a moment that she didn't always feel the need to hesitate. But experience had taught her that throwing caution to the wind rarely turned out well for her.

Still, he'd brought her chocolate for breakfast. Under different circumstances, that would have deserved a kiss.

"Isabella?" Ethan said. "Tell me what you're thinking."

She lowered her gaze, hoping a blush didn't creep up her cheeks.

"I'm thinking you're better in the kitchen than I realized, Ethan. This kind of pastry isn't easy to make. Who taught you?"

He sighed as though caught. "All right. I've taken a few courses at The Seasoned Chef."

Isabella nodded slowly. "Impressive. But please don't tell me you're interested in owning your own restaurant someday."

Ethan shrugged. "I'm a firefighter, Isa. If it weren't for this injury, I'd be suiting up for work every night, just like you."

Isabella finished the pastry. "Well, firefighter or not, you've got talent in the kitchen." She could tell that the praise wasn't lost on him. And that he enjoyed cooking and baking more than he let on. For some reason, the thought bothered her.

"Does chocolate for breakfast warrant something in return?" Ethan asked cautiously.

Isa tensed. "Like what?"

"Three questions answered."

Isa smiled, the tension easing. She liked the fact that he kept surprising her.

"Ask away."

Ethan scooted his chair closer to her and leaned in.

"Do you like me, Isabella Romano?"

Her heart seemed to skip a beat and the intensity in his blue eyes made her want to capture the moment and freeze it. He wouldn't look away. And she was captivated by his straightforwardness.

"Yes," she whispered. He leaned back with a satisfied smile and Isa knew he'd received the answer he'd wanted. She cleared her throat.

"Question number two," she prompted.

"Are you happy?" The serious look in Ethan's eyes didn't waver. Isabella couldn't breathe. She felt as if he were trying to see into her soul, as if he was searching for something.

And what kind of question was that, anyway?

"Why would you ask me that?" she kept her tone restrained, her eyes downward.

"Because I want to know you."

She looked back up at him, unable to resist. "That's a heavy question, Ethan. It's not something I can answer over mediocre coffee in the staff room. But I promise you that I will answer it. When I'm ready."

She liked that he didn't push. His eyes were patient, interested but patient.

"Last question. Will you have dinner with me, Isa?"

Isabella felt her smile start way down inside her and work its way to her face.

"Not yet, Ethan Carter."

His smile corresponded with her own, and Isabella realized that they were evenly matched. He liked the chase. And as much as she tried not to, Isabella liked it, too.

Chapter 4

Ten days had passed since Ethan brought Isabella breakfast. Ten days of chatting and flirting online and a few phone calls, but Isabella hadn't yet relented on a dinner date. The truth was she hadn't had time. Sunday afternoon she stood with her hands on her hips, surveying the situation at her parents' home. She'd agreed to paint the living room for her mother. Her sister-in-law lowered herself to the sofa, her hand rubbing her swollen belly. Isa glanced over at her.

"Mandy?"

Mandy waved her off. "I'm fine. Tired. Uncomfortable. Enormous. But other than that, fine."

Isa knew that at a week past her due date, Mandy wasn't exaggerating. *Uncomfortable* was an understatement.

"I won't be able to help you, Isa," Mandy said apologetically.

"Don't even worry about it. Just try to wait to have the baby until Leo's back from the restaurant."

"Unfortunately, I can probably accomplish that," Mandy lamented. "Tell me about the firefighter."

Isa shrugged. "He brought me chocolate pastries for breakfast last week. He calls me. We chat online a lot. I'm thinking about saying yes to a dinner date."

"You know the fact that he's brought you chocolate pastry is a sign that he's a keeper, right?"

Isa didn't answer. She dipped a roller into the paint in front of her and started painting one of the walls in her parents' living room. Her mother, the consummate decorator, would examine every inch of the wall, no doubt. It had taken time, but Isa had come to realize that her mother's rather newfound need to redecorate parts of her home was in response to her inability to control any part of her husband's health. And as someone who understood the frustration of being unable to control or help, Isa would paint the walls if her mother needed her to.

"You should go into the kitchen, Mandy. I don't want the paint fumes to bother you."

Mandy sighed and pushed herself up. "This little Romano had better make an appearance soon."

"He's an Italian. He'll come when he's ready," Isa said, infusing her words with a flawless Italian accent and animated hand motions. Mandy laughed.

Isa painted until her arms ached and then went to check on her father. The Parkinson's had so affected his body that he stayed mostly at home, venturing out only for doctors' appointments. The medications that had helped restrain his symptoms for some time were starting to wane in their effectiveness. A visiting nurse came every few days to help and a live-in maid did most of the cooking and cleaning for her parents.

She tapped on the bedroom door before poking her head in. Her father reclined on the bed, watching television. His eyes brightened at the sight of Isabella. Isa smiled in response and entered the room.

"Hey, Dad."

He jerked as he nodded at her. As usual, Isa stuffed the ache in her heart as far down as possible, plastering a smile on her face.

She walked to the windows on the far side of the room. The drapes were drawn back and in the distance, Isa could see the mountains. The room was both functional and completely beautiful. Soothing gray and muted yellow filled the space. A soft gray love seat sat tucked into a bay window. Windows, mirrors, vases filled with fresh flowers, a flat-screen television mounted on the wall—her mother had made sure that Gabriel Romano's bedroom was more than comfortable. After enjoying the view, Isa moved to the bed, tucked a blanket over her father's legs and kissed the top of his head.

"Tell me about you, Isa," he said with effort.

"Gladly. It's one of my favorite topics," she said, kicking off her shoes and enjoying the smile that reached her father's eyes. She hopped up on the bed and stole the remote, flipping through channels and talking about work, about Ethan and their breakfast date at the fire station, about everything, because she knew her dad just liked the sound of her voice. Eventually, she looked over and saw that he was asleep. Her throat was dry. She made her way to the kitchen, where her mother was inspecting groceries.

"Ana went shopping. She forgot zucchini."

Isabella opened the refrigerator. "Mom, seriously, just call Leo and ask him to bring some over."

Her mother shook her head. "Mandy left and Leo was meeting her at home. The baby will be here any minute. He needs to stay with her."

Isabella poured a glass of lemonade. "How do you like the living room?"

Her mother washed a cluster of grapes before setting them in a bowl. "Beautiful. The color is perfect. I like the blue." Her mother smiled at her. "Thank you, daughter."

Isabella popped a grape in her mouth. "No problem."

"Tell me about the firefighter," her mother said with a knowing grin.

Isa rolled her eyes. "Who told you? Everyone keeps asking me about him! Why does everyone talk so much in this family?"

"You're one to ask," her mother countered with a chuckle. Isa couldn't think of a comeback.

"Fine. He's really good-looking. He's tall. He likes me. He likes to cook."

Her mother blinked in surprise. "He cooks?"

Isa nodded, taking a handful of grapes. "He used to cook for the firemen. And he bakes. He made me a chocolate croissant and it was fabulous."

"Maybe he's the one," her mother said, almost to herself.

Isa couldn't stop herself from laughing out loud. "Because he can make a fabulous chocolate croissant?"

Her mother didn't answer, but her smile didn't fade.

"Are you ready to find the one?" she asked.

Isa looked at the grapes in her hand. "Maybe."

Her mother leaned over the counter, giving Isa her undivided attention. "Have you ever been in love, Isabella?"

Isa considered the question. She thought over the guys she'd dated since college. A long list of crushes and casual relationships, if they could even be called relationships.

"Over and over, Mom. I fall in love too easily." The admission sent a burst of displeasure through Isa's heart.

"Being in love isn't the same as having a crush or being swept away by emotions. Being in love—and being loved in return—it's like changing directions. And it's okay if you haven't experienced that yet."

"But it's not!" Isa pushed back. "I'm twenty-seven. I've gone out with lots of guys. I've wanted to be married and to be a mother since I played with dolls as a child. Why hasn't that happened for me yet? I love being in love. But it never lasts. There's all this excitement at the beginning. Then it always fizzles. I've never dated someone whom I could really picture myself with for the rest of my life. And even if I could, eventually he couldn't picture himself with me. I'm tired of being disappointed. I'm tired of waiting! And I refuse to keep falling in love so carelessly. Remember Peter? I thought I would marry him."

Her mother bit her lip and Isa knew it was in an attempt to hide a smile. "You were fourteen."

"See? I have a long history of being wrong about guys."

Isabella stood up and walked over to the sink, turning the water on to wash her hands and to avoid eye contact with her mother.

"This isn't what I envisioned for my life. What if I never should have become a nurse?"

"You're a gifted nurse, Isa," her mother told her.

"I keep looking at Mandy and thinking…will I ever have a baby? Will I ever find someone who loves me like Leo loves her?"

Her mother walked over and stood next to her, placing a comforting arm around Isa's shoulders.

"Yes," she answered with calm, tender assurance. "You will. Be patient. Have faith."

Isa didn't respond.

I've been patient. I've had faith. Neither has gotten me where I want to be.

Her thoughts were followed by a stream of guilt. She knew she should have more faith. She wished she could trust without questioning. She wished she could be content with her life.

But her heart fought her. Contentment escaped her. She wanted more.

"I have to go, Mom. I'm working tonight and I need to go home and rest."

Her mother kissed both her cheeks.

"Io sono venuto perché abbiano la vita e l'abbiano in abbondanza."

The words, spoken in Italian, circled Isabella; she wanted to hold on to them, to somehow know they were true.

I am come that they might have life, and that they might have it more abundantly.

The verse was her mother's reminder that Jesus had big wishes for her, too. An abundant life.

"What about Dad?" Isabella's words were barely audible. Her father, a man of great faith, lay weak in the next room. What about his life?

Her mother smoothed Isabella's hair.

"An abundant life isn't necessarily an easy life. But it's beautiful."

At nine-fifty that night, Isabella put her purse and jacket in her locker in the staff room and slammed the locker door shut.

"Easy there, girlfriend."

"Mags, I thought you were off tonight," Isabella said, doing a once-over glance to make sure her friend seemed well. Maggie shrugged.

"Carol asked me to cover her shift and I could use the hours. José and I are trying to save money before the baby comes. Ow!"

"What?" Isabella rushed to her side. Maggie grabbed

Isa's hand and pressed it to the top of her belly. Isabella felt a jab.

"Oh, wow!" Isa grinned as she felt another kick. With her hand pressed to Maggie's belly, feeling the movement of her unborn baby, Isa tried to stifle feelings of longing. The two women walked out to the E.R. together and Isabella thought of how she felt surrounded by pregnant women, an ever-present reminder of the joy of love and marriage—two things that seemed out of her reach. She squelched the ache. Surely her time would come. She thought of her mother.

I need to put my hopes and wishes in God's hands.

If only she could trust that they'd be safe there.

Another stab of guilt pricked her. She pushed away thoughts of God and faith—or lack of faith.

"How's your sister-in-law doing?" Maggie asked.

"They're going to induce in three days."

At the sound of someone crying out for help, both nurses took off running toward the E.R. entrance.

After five hours, two car accident victims, one broken arm, two high fevers and a stomach virus that had resulted in dehydration, the E.R. finally slowed down and Isa checked her cell phone for any messages. She saw one from Ethan. He'd sent it a little before midnight.

Brunch tomorrow? O'Brien's by the firehouse?

Isa couldn't think of a reason to say no. She wanted to see those blue eyes again. And brunch with Ethan would give her something to look forward to for the next few hours. She texted back that she'd meet him there at 10 a.m.

Once her shift ended, Isa rushed home to change, then stopped by her parents' house to check on her dad, checking his vitals and making sure he'd taken his meds. She spoke with the visiting nurse for a few minutes before leaving to meet Ethan. He sat in a small booth by the window and waved her over.

"You're not in your scrubs. I was sort of hoping you'd be wearing the Charlie Brown ones," he mentioned as she slid into the booth across from him.

"So you like seeing me in scrubs," she flirted.

Ethan smiled. "Is that a question?"

"Not really," Isabella answered, and Ethan laughed out loud.

"How was your doctor's appointment this morning?" Isabella asked, watching closely to read Ethan's response. She saw defeat cloud his eyes and she reached across the table to squeeze his hand.

"The doctor said they'll do an X-ray Friday morning to see if the bone has healed and whether I can begin therapy."

"That's a good thing, Ethan. You're making progress."

"I suppose. It's frustrating. I've been wearing this back brace for five weeks. I feel like I've been doing nothing for days and days. Just sitting around, waiting to heal. I'm used to being busy. I'm used to cooking at the firehouse, loading up my gear, rushing out to fight fires or respond to emergencies. This…nothingness…is really getting to me. This isn't who I am."

"You're healing, Ethan. That's what matters. Give it time. And prepare yourself for the physical therapy. It's not going to be as easy as you think."

"You're probably right. But I'm ready and willing to start as soon as I can."

After ordering a plate of scrambled eggs and toast and a cappuccino, Isabella took a good look at the little café.

"So is this where the firefighters hang out? Seems a little dreary to me."

Ethan nodded. "I know. But what do you think about the

location? It's pretty good, right? And what about the size of the restaurant? Not too big but not too small. The kitchen was updated a few months ago, so it's in great shape."

Isabella raised her eyebrows. "Exactly what kind of conversation are we having here? I feel like you're trying to sell me on this hole-in-the-wall café."

Ethan sighed. "It's for sale. The owner wants me to buy it."

Isabella coughed. "Buy it? You want to buy a café? What about the whole fireman thing? Isn't that your career?"

Ethan nodded. "Yes. Absolutely. But look at me, Isa. I'm going crazy at home. I want to be doing something. The restaurant thing… Well, I've always been sort of interested in owning a place like this."

"A dreary place with so-so scrambled eggs and torn vinyl booths?"

Ethan didn't respond. Isabella kept her concentration on her plate of scrambled eggs, trying to understand why she was suddenly feeling so upset. She knew she'd hurt Ethan's feelings. But she'd already told him how she felt about restaurant life. If she'd been hesitant about dating him before, he had to know this wouldn't help. Her cell phone buzzed and she grabbed it, grateful for a distraction from the awkward moment. She gasped at the message.

Baby's coming. Can you meet us at the hospital?

"My sister-in-law is in labor!" Isabella immediately punched in Leo's number and held up her hand for Ethan to wait.

"Leo? How's Mandy?"

"Her water broke and she started having contractions. We're on our way to the hospital. Mandy's nervous."

"I'll meet you at the hospital."

Isabella hung up the phone, her heart pounding. "I have to go, Ethan." She slung her purse over her shoulder.

"Wait! Do you want me to drive over with you or anything?" He looked poised to get up and was already pulling his wallet out to pay for brunch.

She shook her head. "No, that's okay. We could be waiting for hours."

"I don't mind."

"It's a family thing. Mandy would kill me if I introduced you to her ten minutes after she's just given birth. I'll text you to let you know how it's going."

"Oh. Okay, sure. Of course. Keep me posted."

"I will." Isabella paused at the dejected look on Ethan's face. "You know, even if I'm not crazy about restaurant life, that's your choice to make. We'll talk soon, Ethan. I promise."

"I'll be waiting, Isa."

Ethan sat alone in the booth, watching out the window as Isabella ran to her car and sped out of the parking lot. He tried to reason with himself, to talk himself out of feeling hurt by Isa's words.

It's a family thing.

That's your choice to make.

Both comments hit that place in Ethan that always seemed open to being wounded. The inference that he was outside, that his decisions were his alone to make—in short, that he was alone.

Ethan bowed his head at the table.

God, you know that I wish I had a family—parents, siblings, nieces and nephews, people to care about me and bother me and share life with me. That I don't like being alone. That I want someone else to have an opinion about my decisions.

He sipped his coffee, wishing that Isa had let him go to the hospital with her. Wishing that she'd inundate him with questions about his idea of buying a restaurant—or even argue and rant against it. Something. Anything.

It's my decision.

She'd made that clear.

Ethan looked around the café. He could envision the way he would run it. He'd make it a fun place to stop in for breakfast or lunch. Maybe he'd decorate with firefighter memorabilia. He'd create new sandwiches and soups to serve—and chocolate-stuffed croissants for breakfast, of course. He started picturing the revised menu.

I could include my grilled tomato, chicken and cheese sandwich. And that seafood bisque I made last winter that the guys at the station raved about. Maybe my meat-loaf sandwich. Definitely my pulled-pork sandwiches with homemade coleslaw. My cherry-and-cream-cheese Danishes. My peach-cobbler muffins. I need to work on perfecting my corn chowder recipe.

His mind raced with possibilities. As Isa had described it, the little place did look dreary. But Ethan saw potential. He saw a warm café, brimming with people, with food, friends and life. The truth was that he'd already made inquiries at the bank. He knew he could most likely secure a loan.

He slowly stood up and made his way to the back where Mick kept his office. He tapped on the door.

"Come in!"

Ethan poked his head in. "Mick, can we talk?"

Mick's eyes lit up with hope as he sat in the most cluttered office that Ethan had ever seen.

"I hope you're here to tell me I'll be going to Alaska soon."

Ethan took a deep breath. He made his decision.

"Tell Miss Kay to start packing."

Chapter 5

Isabella jogged down the hospital corridor toward Mandy's room. She knocked and pushed open the door. Leo stood in front of the television flipping through channels, and Mandy lay in the hospital bed munching on ice chips.

"What's going on here?" Isabella put her hands on her hips. "I thought we were having a baby!"

Leo chuckled. "The contractions have slowed. They're talking about giving her Pitocin to move things along."

Isabella moved to Mandy's side and squeezed her hand. "Hey, sis. How are you?"

Mandy bit her lip.

Afraid, Isabella thought to herself.

"I'm not sure whether I want things to hurry up or slow down."

Isabella perched herself on the side of the bed. "You want things to hurry up, Mandy. Trust me. Can't you just imagine that little Romano in your arms?"

Mandy smiled at that, though the nervousness didn't leave her eyes. "I am anxious to hold him. I wonder if he has hair."

Isabella laughed. "Look at your husband. There's a good chance." Both girls looked at Leo's full head of jet-black hair and giggled together.

"My parents are on their way from Evergreen," Mandy commented.

"Want me to make sure they stay in the waiting room?" Isabella whispered, knowing Mandy's mother's tendency to want to take control.

Before Mandy could answer, she scrunched her eyes closed and groaned. Leo was back by her side in a flash.

"Contraction?" he asked, and Mandy grunted a yes, not opening her eyes.

"Almost over, Mandy," Isa said, watching the monitor. "Baby Romano will be here before you know it."

Four hours later Isa held her new nephew, Antonio Gabriel Romano, in her arms. At eight pounds and nine ounces with a headful of black hair, Antonio had stolen his aunt's heart. Isa rocked him in her arms. The recovery room was full. Mandy's parents and brother and sister-in-law hovered around Isa as she held the baby, and Isa's own mother stood fussing over Mandy, with Leo next to her, beaming like the proud papa he was. Reluctantly, Isa handed baby Tony to Mandy's mother. Her phone buzzed and she stepped outside to the hallway to answer it.

"Hi, Ethan!"

"Are you an auntie?"

Isa smiled, leaning back against the wall. "Yes. We say *la zia* for *aunt* in Italian. Tony is gorgeous. Mandy was incredible. She was afraid at first, but she ended up having to help calm Leo down. He nearly fainted."

Ethan laughed. "Were you in the room with them?"

"Yes. Leo was so jittery when it was time to push that Mandy insisted I stay for support in case we lost him."

"Will you be staying all night?"

"No." Isabella yawned. "Leo's staying with Mandy. I'm going home to sleep until my shift at ten. I'll come back tomorrow. I can't believe I'm an aunt!"

"Was that the first birth you've attended?" Ethan asked.

"My fifth. I have a lot of cousins, Ethan. Plus I assisted on a delivery in the E.R. during my first year as a nurse. What about you? Have you ever had to deliver a baby? I've heard of firefighters having to do that during emergencies."

"No, thankfully. I'd be terrified. The only time I want to be involved in a birth is when my own baby is being born."

Isa didn't answer for a moment, her pulse leaping at the direction of the conversation.

"Do labor and delivery frighten you at all?" Ethan asked. Through the door, Isa could hear Tony cry and an immediate chorus of concerned voices. She smiled at the sound.

"No," she answered. "The prize at the end is worth it."

The door cracked open and her mother motioned for her to come back. "I have to go, Ethan. Call me tomorrow."

"I will."

Isa hung up the phone, but she couldn't quite get Ethan's words out of her head. The reality that he wanted children hovered in her thoughts.

He didn't say if. *He said* when. *He wants kids. Good to know.*

The next morning, Isa planned to leave the E.R. at 6:00 a.m. and make her way up to the fourth level of the hospital. She wouldn't deny that she'd taken every one of her breaks up in the maternity ward overnight. It was convenient working just an elevator ride away from her new nephew. After the exhaustion of giving birth, Mandy had chosen for Tony to sleep in the nursery, waking up every few hours to nurse. Isabella had been thrilled to be so near the new baby.

She knew she'd need to head home for sleep soon or she would collapse from exhaustion, but she wanted just one more snuggle with Tony. She grabbed a cup of coffee from the staff room and her purse.

"You know that's not going to be strong enough, Isa."

Isabella swirled around.

"Ethan! How did you get in here?"

He grinned and leaned against the doorframe. "Maggie."

"How did you bribe her?" Isa asked, eyeing the paper bag in his arms. He laughed.

"Breakfast. Listen, I don't want to hold you up. I figured you were going up to the maternity ward. I thought I'd bring breakfast for your family."

"You brought breakfast for Leo and Mandy, too?" Isa asked, her heart softening.

"Yeah, well, cooking is my outlet for boredom. You know I'm used to working nights."

"I know," Isa said, moving forward and peeking in the bag. The smell of bacon made her stomach growl. "Are those homemade biscuits? You're spoiling me," she commented.

"I'm trying. And of course they are. It's my first attempt to impress your family. So you've got homemade biscuits layered with maple bacon, melted cheddar cheese and butter-fried eggs."

"Mmmm. It smells great, Ethan." Isa took the bag from his arms. "So do you want to come up with me?"

He paused and Isa thought he looked stunned by the invitation. "I do, but it's early and they might be sleeping."

She nodded. "Thank you for breakfast, Ethan. You certainly know the way to a girl's heart. This was really thoughtful." They were quiet for a moment, with the smells of warm, buttery biscuits and maple bacon floating between them.

"Did you decide what to do about the café?" Isa made herself ask.

He looked down at his shoes. "Sort of."

"You're buying it, aren't you?" Isa said, hoping she was able to mask the disappointment she felt. But one look at Ethan told her it had registered.

"I want to, Isabella," he answered in a quiet voice. "Could we get together soon to talk about it?"

She clutched the paper bag. "We don't have to talk about it, Ethan. It's your decision."

She saw annoyance flicker across his eyes. "I know that. But I'd like to explain some things to you."

She didn't mind the tension in his tone. If anything, the slight change intrigued Isabella. She nodded. "Okay. The next few days are really hectic for me, Ethan. And I want to be available to help Mandy and Leo as much as possible. So how about dinner Friday night?"

She almost laughed at how quickly the annoyance in his eyes was replaced with astonishment.

"Seriously? I'm graduating from the breakfast-and-lunch-date circuit?"

"It's on a trial basis, tough guy. Don't get ahead of yourself."

"I'll take what I can get," he said with a chuckle. "Friday. Let me know how breakfast tastes, okay?"

"Oh, I will," Isabella said playfully, smiling as he walked away.

She headed up to Mandy's room, pleased to find everyone awake. Mandy sat on the bed nursing Tony while Leo worked on his laptop. He jumped up at the smell of breakfast sandwiches, digging into the bag while Isabella relayed the story of Ethan bringing made-from-scratch biscuits.

"No one told me that your fireman can cook!" Mandy said as she lifted Tony to her shoulder and gently patted him on the back.

"He's not my fireman. But yes, he's got skills."

Leo took a giant bite of a sandwich and closed his eyes. "I have to agree," he said after swallowing. "That's delicious."

"Really?" Mandy raised an eyebrow. Isa knew that as a respected food critic and writer for *Denver Lifestyle Magazine,* Mandy held very high standards for food.

"As good as Myra's Coffee House, Mandy," Leo assured her.

"Here, hand over Tony so you can eat," Isa insisted. She took her nephew and Leo handed Mandy a sandwich.

Isa walked with Tony over to the window, where she could see a light rain beginning to fall. The feeling of such a tiny baby in her arms filled her with contentment.

"Well?" she asked once Mandy had eaten half her sandwich.

"In my professional opinion? We've got a perfectly light, buttery, flaky biscuit that crumbles like I like them to. Strong melted cheddar and absolutely delicious maple bacon, just crispy enough to add crunch but still with plenty of flavor. But it's the fried egg that brings this all together into one wonderful breakfast sandwich. This guy should be in the food business."

Isabella sighed. "I was afraid you'd say that."

Chapter 6

Late Friday afternoon Ethan looked at the faded sign of
O'Brien's. Despite the affection Company 51 had for the old
café, he could readily admit the place needed some work.

"You just bought yourself a café!" Caleb said with a fist
pump in the air. The two men stood across the street from
the building, taking in the sight of Ethan's newest purchase.

"I must be crazy. What was I thinking?" Ethan felt nau-
seated. Caleb howled with laughter.

"You were thinking you needed something to do until
you're back at the fire station, and this is it. Maybe it will
take off and you'll be a rich man."

Ethan gave Caleb a doubtful look. "Most likely I'll be
a very poor man."

"Hey, think positively! You prayed about this, right?"

Ethan nodded. "Yes. But it was a fast decision. And you
know I'm still new to this. I wasn't sure how I was supposed
to know that God was for it or not."

"You mean He didn't send you an email?" Caleb gasped, and Ethan rolled his eyes.

"No. Like you've told me before, I prayed and tried to listen for that still, small voice in my heart."

"And you felt good about moving forward with the purchase?"

"At the time. Right now I'm feeling massive amounts of anxiety."

"Totally normal. Let's go inside, man. Mick's last day is today, right?"

"No, he's going to train me for two weeks. I've got so much to learn—buying the food, payroll, maintenance, overhead, marketing. I wish I'd paid more attention to the business classes I took back in college. I know it will take more than two weeks for me to learn the business, but I'm going to give it my best shot and learn as much as I can. I'm starting from scratch and it could be a disaster."

"It's going to be fine. You can do this. So should we go in?"

"Nah, I can't right now. I'm meeting Isabella for dinner later and I don't want to be late."

"Dinner? Really? Finally?" Caleb said in mock amazement.

"Yeah, yeah. I know. I don't think I've ever pursued a woman like this before. I'm cooking for her, Caleb."

Caleb grinned. "The girl has you wrapped around her finger."

Ethan shrugged. "You've met her. She's worth the effort."

"Agreed. Did you tell her you signed the papers on O'Brien's this afternoon?"

"It's not really O'Brien's anymore. I'm changing the name," Ethan told him. "And no, I haven't told her. She's not a big fan of restaurant ownership. I'm a little worried she'll back off if I tell her that I bought a café."

"Tell her. You never know—maybe she'll have some good advice for you."

"I have a feeling her advice would be for me to run as fast as I can in the opposite direction from the café."

"Which isn't very fast these days. How's your back?"

"Well, I had the X-ray at nine this morning and my doctor said that I can begin therapy next Monday. That's a step in the right direction. Finally! I'm so sick of wearing this back brace." Ethan refrained from going into detail about how the thought of therapy made him anxious and he still felt pain at times.

"Good news! I'm praying for you, buddy. Hang in there. I better get back to the station. And you know all of 51 is behind you with this café. It's going to be great."

"Let's hope so."

Ethan climbed up in his truck, as usual wincing from the soreness in his back, and headed closer to downtown to meet Isabella at a Brazilian steak house for dinner. Isabella's choice. They sat in a booth near the front window and chatted about Ethan beginning physical therapy and Isa's family's adoration for new baby Tony. While their waiter shaved delicate, flavorful pieces of meat onto their plates, Isa gushed about how fun it was to have a new baby in the family, and Ethan gathered up the courage to tell her about the café.

"You're just now telling me you bought the café?" she said in disbelief once he admitted that he'd signed the papers and O'Brien's now belonged to him.

"I wasn't sure I could get the loan. I didn't want to tell you until I knew I was going to do this. And honestly, I thought it would take longer for the loan to go through and everything. Everything just fell into place and happened really quickly."

"I see."

Ethan hated that Isabella could be so hard to read. He had no idea of what she was thinking. Was she angry? Frustrated? Planning her exit strategy from his life?

"Tell me why you want to own a café," she said finally.

He breathed relief. That he could do. For the next half hour, he told her all about his experience at the diner and his vision for the café.

"Owning my own restaurant was a dream I had when I was younger. Then I threw myself into being a firefighter and thought that the time had passed for the possibility that I might run my own restaurant. And I was okay with that, really. Being a firefighter is such a part of who I am. It was easy to give up on the idea of owning a restaurant. But now…I sort of feel like this is my second chance at that dream.

"I'm not giving up on being a firefighter, Isa. It's only breakfast and lunch. I'm still planning to go back to Company 51. I'm not sure what my schedule will look like, but I'll hire some help at the café. And the fact that it's next door to the firehouse is obviously convenient for me. Mick's going to take two weeks to train me in running the café, the bookkeeping and the purchasing. I'm realizing how much there is to learn," he concluded. "I plan to serve *pain au chocolat,* by the way."

"Well, that's something," Isabella teased. Ethan loved the way she looked whenever she teased him. The light in her eyes and the good-natured ease in her manner—definitely two of Isabella's best qualities.

Ethan took in every aspect of her as she talked. Her mannerisms, the way she shook back her thick, wavy hair, the way she always seemed to wear dangly earrings and how great they looked on her. He wondered if she felt the attraction as strongly as he did. With every moment, every word spoken, Ethan felt more drawn to her.

She's like a light. And I just keep wanting to be as close to her as possible. I'm not sure she even realizes it.

"Leo makes this cherry cassata torte—it's incredible. You should try it."

"I was wondering…" Ethan broached the subject warily. "Any chance I could meet this brother you talk about all the time? I know Leo and Mandy are preoccupied with the baby right now. But whenever it's a good time, I'd like to meet them."

Ethan found it to be a good sign that Isabella just looked at him in that thoughtful way she did sometimes, when he knew she was contemplating what he'd just said.

"So you really want to meet my family?"

"More than you know," Ethan answered.

"And you think you're ready for the Romanos?"

"Absolutely."

"You haven't said much about your family, Ethan," Isabella said, curiosity in her voice.

I suppose I can't expect her to give me her history if I won't share mine.

Ethan folded his hands on the table. "I've mentioned before that my parents both died when I was in college. I was a late child. My parents spent much of their early married life trying to get pregnant with no luck. It wasn't until several years after they'd given up that I came along. My mom was forty-five."

"You were a late blessing," Isabella surmised.

"That's a nice way to say it, Isabella. Thank you. I was definitely a surprise. My father died of a heart attack my first year of college. He and I were never very close, though. He worked a lot running a construction company. My mom died of cancer two years after that. Neither of my parents had siblings. And I never knew my grandparents."

"No cousins? No aunts and uncles? No, I guess not if your parents were only children."

Ethan shook his head. Isabella's expression communicated clearly her sadness for him but Ethan just shrugged.

"It was okay. And now—God helps fill the void. I only wish I'd discovered my faith earlier. It's made all the difference. Especially now."

Isabella's gaze drifted toward the window and the busy street in front of the restaurant.

"But I did always wish I had siblings," Ethan continued, not wanting to press her on the subject of faith.

"Is that why you became a firefighter?" Isabella rested her chin on the palms of her hands.

"One of the reasons, I suppose. The camaraderie definitely appealed to me. I also really like the hats."

Isabella laughed and Ethan grinned along with her.

"Was your mother a good cook?" Isabella asked.

Ethan paused while their waiter refilled their glasses of water.

"Not really. She didn't cook much. I grew up eating a lot of frozen dinners." He laughed at Isa's look of consternation. "Not everyone grew up with the famous Gabriel Romano cooking for them, you know."

"So how did you fall in love with cooking?" Isa wondered.

"In high school my best friend lived down the street from me. His mother was a terrific cook. I spent a lot of evenings at their house. She cooked a lot of all-American meals. You know, meat loaf, cheeseburgers, pot roast and potatoes, chicken casserole. I realized that there was more to life than frozen Stroganoff."

Isa gave him a small smile of understanding. She was quiet and Ethan waited for her to speak.

"I have a big family, Ethan," Isabella said after a moment, her voice pensive. Ethan leaned closer with the anticipation that she wanted to share more with him. "My family means everything to me. We're close. There's drama. Everyone has an opinion about everything—but we're all there for each other. I would like you to meet them, but I'm afraid you'll be overwhelmed by the chaos that inevitably comes with my family get-togethers."

Ethan grinned. "Are you kidding? I like chaos. I need more chaos in my life."

"You're sure about that?"

"Absolutely."

"In that case, Ethan Carter, you're invited to the Romano family dinner Monday night."

"Can José make it to family dinner, too?" Isabella asked Maggie. Isabella stood with her clipboard while Maggie sat on a stool, carefully giving a twelve-year-old stitches for a minor skateboard accident.

"Are you kidding? Dinner with your family? He wouldn't miss it. I stopped cooking the moment I found out I was pregnant. He'll be salivating at the thought of a home-cooked meal. And Fireman Ethan is coming, too, huh? This should be fun."

"Pishposh," Isa said, pretending to brush off her friend's comments. Maggie took a breath and sat back for a moment.

"Mags, everything okay?" Isa instantly asked.

"Isa, I'm seven months pregnant. At any given moment I'm having heartburn, being kicked from the inside or needing to empty my bladder." She glanced up from her stitching. "I'm fine."

Isa nodded. "But you're on your feet so much. You need to go straight home and sleep until late afternoon," she instructed.

"You don't have to tell me twice. That's my plan. You need to, as well. Those dark circles under your eyes need some attention."

Isa stretched and twisted back and forth to loosen her stiff muscles. "True. I'll see you both tonight at my parents' house around seven, okay?"

"We'll be there. But I'm not offering to bring anything. I'm pregnant, remember?"

Isa grinned. "There will be enough food for an army. I told my mother I'm bringing a date. Trust me, she's going all out. It's her way of trying to help her poor single daughter catch a husband. I didn't offer to bring anything, either."

Maggie laughed. "I love your family. See you tonight, Isa."

Ethan stood nervously outside the Romano family home, holding a bouquet of flowers for Isa's mother, the hostess of the evening. The door opened and Isa stood in front of him. She cocked her head to the side.

"Are those for me?"

"Only if you'll share them with your mother," he answered. Isa smiled as though she'd expected his answer.

"She'll love you forever," Isa said.

"That's what I'm hoping." Ethan stepped inside. The house was loud. He came to a stop in the foyer, absorbing the sounds and smells of a house so filled with life. He could hear music playing in the distance and raised voices speaking in both Italian and English. The house smelled of chicken, tomatoes, garlic, onion and olive oil. Children raced past Ethan and clambered up the stairs, yelling about who would get to play video games first.

"How was therapy this morning?" Isa asked.

Ethan shrugged. "It went fairly well. I'll be going twice a week or more for a while."

The visit had consisted of his therapist, Isaac, doing an evaluation and discussing the plan for Ethan's therapy treatment. Ethan had liked both Isaac and Keira, the physical-therapist assistant. So he at least felt positive about working with them for the next several weeks. Ethan didn't mention to Isa that he'd experienced some pain in the initial biomechanics and muscle-strength testing, which Isaac had noted and which had discouraged Ethan.

He slowly followed Isa down the hallway. The far side of the kitchen had large windows that flanked French doors. The doors opened to a huge deck where a group of people mingled, some sitting at an outdoor table. A woman who Ethan assumed was Isa's sister-in-law sat on a swing, a swaddled baby in her arms. Another pregnant woman joined her on the swing.

"Maggie?" Ethan said in surprise. Isa nodded.

"She and her husband, José, have sort of joined our family. Maggie's family lives way out on the East Coast. She moved out here years ago to go to college and then met and fell in love with José. The Romanos have made her an honorary member," Isabella told him, and then introduced him to her mother, who smiled with pleasure when she accepted the flowers.

He was introduced to so many people that Ethan knew he'd never be able to remember them all. But one person in particular, Ethan knew he'd remember. Gabriel Romano sat in an easy chair placed in the kitchen just for him. Having met people with Parkinson's before, Ethan wasn't at all alarmed or uncomfortable with the way Gabriel shook almost constantly. Ethan took Gabriel's hand gently in his own, noticing how attentive Isabella was to her father.

"Isa! Isa!"

The room went silent in one fell swoop at the sound of

someone screaming Isa's name. Ethan and Isabella turned in sync, both rushing out to the deck.

A man Ethan assumed to be Isa's brother—the family resemblance was obvious—and another he assumed to be Maggie's husband were cradling Maggie on the floor of the deck.

"Move!" Isa commanded to the others hovering around them. Ethan joined her as they knelt down on the deck. Cold fear filled Isa's eyes at the sight of Maggie's insipid face and the blood trickling down to her ankles.

"Mags?"

Maggie moaned, her eyes half-closed. "Some—something's wrong," she said, her hand reaching down to clutch her belly. "Isa, help...."

Ethan immediately pressed his fingers to Maggie's wrist. "Pulse is weak," he said to Isa. "How far along is she?"

"Twenty-eight or twenty-nine weeks—I'm not positive. She's miscarried before, but this pregnancy has been normal so far." Isa's voice wavered.

"We need to get her to the hospital," Ethan said definitively.

"I've got 911 on the phone!" someone yelled out.

"Tell them we need an ambulance!" Isa said before taking Maggie's face in her hands. Ethan could feel Isabella start to shake beside him.

"The hospital is close. Let's just drive her," he said, knowing by the look of things that every minute was crucial. "We need towels," he said to Leo, who jumped up and ran into the house. "Can you carry her?" he asked her husband.

"Maggie, can you hear me?" Isa waved for everyone to move even farther back. "Clear the area, you guys." Isa hiked up Maggie's dress to examine her. Leo came rushing back with towels.

Ethan hated feeling so trapped by his injury. Under normal circumstances, he could scoop Maggie up and carry her to the car. But her husband lifted her with the help of Leo.

"Has she been having contractions?" Ethan asked as they all rushed out to the front yard. José shook his head, his face terrified.

"Not that I know of. She was feeling a little discomfort in the car, but she didn't say much about it. It's too early." He choked on the last words.

"The baby," Maggie cried suddenly. "Don't let me lose her. Please." It was a low, guttural plea, and Ethan watched as tears streamed down Isa's face. Ethan had been through enough emergency situations to know to disregard his rising panic and concentrate on the moment at hand. He steadied himself, praying inwardly for strength.

"It's going to be okay, Maggie," Isa said amid her tears. Ethan could sense her trying to hold herself together. They piled into Leo's Suburban, with Leo at the wheel. In the back, Ethan and Isa used the towels to absorb the blood. Ethan kept checking Maggie's pulse. He pulled out his cell phone and speed-dialed Caleb's number, then told him in clipped sentences to let the hospital know they were coming.

"Maggie," he said calmly. He leaned over her, talking to her constantly, reassuring her. Every bump in the road felt magnified as Leo drove as fast as he could to the hospital. Ethan could see Maggie's husband crying in the front seat. Maggie gripped Ethan's hand.

"Pray, Isa," Leo said firmly from the driver's seat.

Isabella blinked, tears still falling. "God, please help us. Please help Maggie and this baby. Please help…. Please do something! Do something! Why are You letting this happen? Don't You see us? Do something!" Her frantic voice rose to a yell.

"Isa," Ethan interjected, his steady voice covering hers. She gulped a breath and they just stared at each other. There in the car, both holding her bleeding friend, Ethan watched Isa fall apart. She took a ragged breath and shook her head as more tears streamed down her face.

"Isa," Ethan's tone was measured on purpose. She latched on to his gaze and didn't look away. "We can do this. We can get Maggie through this together. I'm here with you. Okay, Isa?"

She just stared at him, absorbing his words.

"Maggie, we're almost there. It's going to be all right," Ethan encouraged. Maggie, wide-eyed with fear now, gripped Ethan's hand. He squeezed back firmly. "I'm here. José's here. Isa's here. God is here. Maggie, we'll be at the hospital soon and they'll take care of you and your baby."

"God is here," Maggie whispered. Ethan nodded with more assurance than he felt.

"We're here!" Leo swerved into the E.R. entrance. The passenger door was opened the moment the Suburban stopped, a team of people waiting with a stretcher.

"Isa! Status!" one person demanded. Isa seemed to reclaim her control. She wiped her face as she hopped from the car. "Maggie Sanchez, thirty-two years old, seven months pregnant…"

Ethan followed quickly with José as Isa updated the team. They rushed Maggie immediately to the maternity ward. Ethan was joined by Leo in the waiting room as José and Isa disappeared down the hallway.

"Do you think she'll be all right?" Leo asked.

"Even if they have to deliver at seven months, the baby

could make it. I don't know. It depends on what's wrong. I wish I knew her history."

Both were quiet for a moment. Ethan felt his heart pounding in his chest. He thought of Isabella crying, the desperate tone in her voice, the frantic look in her eyes.

"In the car, I know Isa was…" Leo began to speak but his words trailed off.

"I wish I knew *her* history, too." Ethan said, his eyes glued to the closed doors in front of them.

Leo nodded. "Sit down with me."

Chapter 7

Ethan and Leo jumped from their seats as Isa pushed through the doors to the waiting room. An hour and a half had flown by since they'd rushed into the E.R. Deep in conversation with Leo, Ethan had hardly noticed the time. Darkness covered the windows in the waiting room.

Isa's clothes were still caked with Maggie's blood. Ethan wasn't sure whether to take her in his arms or give her space. He didn't have to decide. Isa walked up to him and threw her arms around him. Leo unobtrusively stepped aside. Ethan rubbed her back, murmuring words of comfort. Isa buried her face into his chest and gripped the back of his shirt.

She finally pulled away, wiping fresh tears from her eyes. Ethan wanted so badly to pull her back, to kiss the tears from her eyes. Her petite frame seemed frail and weary.

"Maggie?" Ethan was afraid to ask, but Isa just inhaled and nodded.

"The baby?" Leo asked.

"Two pounds, three ounces. Emergency Cesarean section."

"She had the baby?" Leo said with shock.

"There was no choice. The baby was in distress and Maggie was losing too much blood. The baby is small. Her lungs aren't fully developed yet. But they think she'll be all right. She won't be able to leave the hospital for weeks. Maggie's been through a lot tonight. She's resting now."

Leo's cell phone rang and he walked into the hallway to answer it. Ethan sat down and pulled Isa next to him.

"What happened?" he asked.

"Cervical insufficiency. It's pretty rare, but it usually results in late-term miscarriages or preterm births. I'm just so thankful that the baby's going to be okay, that we made it here in time. Maggie would have been so devastated—" Isa's voice broke. Ethan pulled her close to him.

"Hey, everything's going to be okay," he told her softly.

"I'm so glad you were there, Ethan. I was losing it and you were calm."

He kept his arm around her. "We were both worried. That's okay. You know that comes with the job." She looked up at him with tear-filled eyes and Ethan's heart lurched. Without even thinking, he leaned forward and kissed her tenderly. It was a quick kiss, and Ethan hoped against hope that it hadn't been a mistake. Isa just blinked in surprise. Then she framed his face with her hands and kissed him back.

Ethan's breath caught in his throat at the restrained kiss. It was a gentle kiss but so much smoldered beneath it. If he'd ever wondered whether Isa returned the attraction that he felt for her, he didn't doubt it at that moment.

"Isa."

She jumped at the sound of her brother's voice.

Not now, Leo, Ethan thought to himself with a silent

growl. He looked over at Leo, who looked appropriately embarrassed and held out a phone.

"José's sister called. His family wants an update."

Isa took the phone. "Of course."

Ethan sat silently as Isa explained what had happened to Maggie and assured José's family that both Maggie and the baby were stable and being monitored closely. With one hand she held the cell phone to her ear. Ethan reached over and took her other hand, lacing their fingers together.

Isabella dropped her purse and kicked off her shoes the minute she entered her apartment, utterly spent. She'd stayed at the hospital to be with Maggie until José's family had been able to arrive from Pueblo, Colorado. Once Maggie and José had family there to support them, Isabella had allowed Leo to drive her home. She'd insisted Ethan go home earlier. Sitting in the waiting room, his back had grown taut and Isa could see he was in pain. She'd been adamant in her wish that he go home and take his pain medication.

After a hot shower, she changed into sweatpants and a T-shirt, then made her way to the sofa and lay down, covering herself with a fleece blanket. As he'd dropped her off, Leo had ordered her to get some sleep. While at the hospital, Isa had texted friends until she'd found someone to take her shift for that night. Now lying on the sofa, she closed her heavy eyes, falling into a desperately needed deep slumber.

When she woke hours later, Isa sat up stiffly, blinking to see the clock above her mantle.

Four in the morning.

She grumbled while wrapping her blanket around her and shuffling to her bedroom. But once settled in her soft bed, tucked under a down comforter, she couldn't turn her mind off. Her eyes adjusted to the darkness and she stared up at the ceiling, reliving the previous day's events. She could hear someone screaming her name, feel the sense of fright that ran through her at seeing Maggie collapsed on the ground; she remembered the helplessness she felt during the ride to the hospital.

Isa's throat went dry at the memory of her prayer, which probably came across as more of a tirade. She felt a twinge of embarrassment at how she'd lost control of her emotions. And she wondered what Ethan thought of the whole situation. Thoughts of Ethan were inevitably followed by thoughts of the kiss they'd shared in the waiting room.

Isa touched her lips.

She knew she'd been overwhelmed at that moment and that the kiss had been a result of all the intense emotion welling up within both of them. That hardly seemed to matter. Whether it was fueled by intense circumstances or not, Isabella knew one thing—the feelings that came with his kiss scared her. It was a kiss filled with desire, affection, possibly even love.

The reality that she might be falling in love with Ethan hit her full force.

Don't do this to yourself again. She sighed in frustration at the warring emotions in her and proceeded to scold herself. *Who knows if it's real? Who knows if Ethan feels the same? Or if he will six months from now? You always do this. Don't lose your head and your heart over one kiss.*

But it was *one incredible kiss.*

Isa's thoughts went back to her prayer-turned-rant during the car ride. She sat up, pushing her pillows behind her and drawing her knees to her chin. In the absolute stillness and silence of her apartment, with a slightly calmer spirit, she felt the need to continue the conversation, not with Ethan but the One she'd been so angry with.

I was so afraid for Maggie, Father.

A tug to tell the whole truth came from within her.

I'm afraid for my dad. I'm afraid he won't be here when I finally get married. I'm afraid he won't be here when I finally have children. I'm afraid my family will change forever when we lose him and I'll never be happy again. We've already lost the man he once was, but I can deal with that. He's still my dad, and I'm still his little girl—that won't change. But I've prayed a million prayers as his health has deteriorated, and they haven't changed anything. I've prayed and I've asked and I've waited and I've hoped. Nothing happens. Today when I prayed for Maggie, I couldn't bear the thought that again I would call out to You, and again nothing would happen.

One more strong pull for more caused Isabella to close her eyes in confession.

"I'm afraid I can't trust You." The words came out in a whisper.

Isa's chin quivered at that final, so very honest admission. She bowed her head until her forehead rested on her knees, and she wept. Deep tears that she'd pushed down now rose to the surface, unable to be ignored. She cried until there seemed to be no tears left. Then she lay curled on her side. She had strength left for one last prayer.

Help me trust You when I don't know how.

At 5:00 a.m. on Tuesday morning, Ethan walked through the kitchen of his newly purchased café. The keys felt heavy in his pocket as the weight of the purchase settled on his shoulders.

God, please help me do this. Being here feels right, but I know I can't do it without You.

The smell of bread baking wafted through the kitchen. Ethan knew Mick would be arriving at seven. Ethan would shadow his every move for the next few days, hoping to get a handle on the ropes of the business. Starting the following week, Ethan would close shop for a few weeks to redecorate and start fresh, but Mick would continue training him on the management side of the business, even while the café dining room was updated and redesigned. The employees had been told of the change in ownership. Ethan had been blunt about what he expected from his new staff and had given them the choice to stay or go. Upon hearing his expectations and requirements, only one part-time assistant cook, Carson, and one waitress, Jenny, had decided to stay. Ethan would begin an immediate search for new waitstaff and another cook in the meantime. He planned to run his own kitchen as much as possible. The thought of cooking for customers both excited and terrified him.

Alarm raced through him at the enormity of his new responsibilities. Ethan left the kitchen and walked through the dining room, studying the room and considering where he wanted to make changes. One of the firefighters was married to an interior designer. Ethan had asked her to meet with him and come up with a plan for redecorating the interior. He hoped Mick would have some ideas on marketing, although the café had been going downhill for some time. Maybe Mick wasn't the best person to ask. But if she were willing, Ethan had no doubt that Isabella would have ideas for him.

That is, if she wanted to continue dating him now that he was in the restaurant business.

Ethan sat at the coffee bar, thinking over the ordeal that had happened at the Romanos' family dinner. Despite the stress of the situation, he'd been glad to be by Isa's side through all of it.

As they'd sat together at the hospital, Leo had shed some light on Isa's tendency to put up defenses and hold back.

Parts of their discussion had particularly stuck in Ethan's mind. He kept replaying one specific exchange with Leo. When Ethan asked why Isa seemed so unwilling to give their relationship a chance, Leo had thought for several moments before finally answering.

"Isa's experience with love has been that it's never real. Sparks fly and then fade. I don't think she trusts herself to know lasting love from fleeting romance. And she's just not interested in the latter anymore."

Ethan had pressed for answers.

"What about her faith in God?" he'd asked Leo.

Leo had hesitated before finally answering.

"Isabella is a visual, passionate, often impulsive woman. Understand me when I say that those are beautiful qualities that make my sister who she is—but for a visual, passionate woman, an invisible God who speaks in a still, small, mysterious way...well, it's like any relationship, I suppose—she's not sure she can trust Him when she doesn't feel that He cares for her in tangible ways."

Ethan had pondered Leo's answer well into the night. As someone who had come to faith later in life and could only wish he'd had Jesus to turn to from childhood, he struggled to understand Isa's disillusionment. A knock at the glass door of the café made Ethan jolt. Caleb stood there waving at him. Ethan walked over and unlocked the door.

"I was about to start my shift when I saw your truck out front. Still feeling anxious?" Caleb asked.

Ethan motioned for him to take a seat at the coffee bar with him.

"Yes. But I'm fairly confident this was the right decision. And now that I've made it, I'm ready to dive in headfirst. I want to make this work."

"Good." Caleb nodded. "But don't get too comfortable—we want you back at the station."

Ethan smiled. "Thanks. Don't worry. I miss fighting fires too much to let it go."

"The doc cleared you for therapy, right?" Caleb asked, and Ethan brightened.

"Yeah. I started Monday."

"How was it?"

Ethan shrugged. "Not too bad. They went easy on me since it was my first time. But Isaac, my therapist, warned me it's not going to be easy. I need to strengthen my core. I have a feeling the exercises will be painful. I'm ready, though. I want to get back to the way that I was."

"Don't push it too hard, man. Now with the café…well, you've got a lot weighing on you. Take it one day at a time."

After a moment, Ethan decided to share with Caleb his concern for Isabella. After all, it had been Caleb who had introduced him to Christ. Ethan figured he might have some insight. Caleb listened intently, stroking his chin.

"The thing about faith, Ethan, is that it's not always easy. It sounds to me as though faith has been a part of Isabella's life for a long time. When unfortunate things happen, or things that are out of our control, as Christians we turn to God. But when we turn to Him and never seem to get an answer—or the answer always seems to be no— that can cause anyone to feel disappointed.

"All of us go through times when we wonder whether our prayers are going beyond the ceiling. Life throws curves at us. It can be hard to have faith when nothing seems to go right. A relationship with God can be much like any relationship with someone you love. The passion can grow cold. The trust and deep love can falter at times—at least, on our side it can. Not on God's side. God hasn't abandoned Isabella, Ethan. Sometimes you might feel like you have faith to move mountains. Other times you might question whether you have faith to keep believing. It sounds like Isa's struggling to keep believing right now."

"What can I do?" Ethan clasped his hands on the table.

"Support her. Encourage her. Be her friend. Pray for her." Caleb smiled. "I've learned from my wife that when a woman has lost her passion, she usually needs to feel pursued."

"You're saying I should pursue her?" Ethan asked.

Caleb shook his head. "No. You already are, buddy. She wants to feel God pursue her."

Chapter 8

Isa walked through the door of Ethan's café, halting at the destruction zone in front of her. The flooring had been ripped up and half the room had been painted a different color. Some sort of contraption was being built in the center of the room. Ethan had definitely jumped in with both feet when it came to redesign. A little more than a week had passed since he'd closed the café and everything looked like a royal mess.

"Isa!" Ethan came through the kitchen with a wide smile on his face. "Welcome to my café!"

"Thanks. It's looking…um… Is *demolished* a nice way to say what I'm thinking?"

Ethan laughed. "Demo is an accurate description," he agreed. "But it won't be this way much longer. Couple more days until the walls are completely painted. Then the floors will go in. The guys have been stopping over between shifts, helping paint and ripping up the floor. I think they like being destructive. Even the chief was over here earlier, painting. Rachel's shopping for new decor as we speak."

"Rachel?" Isa raised her eyebrows.

"Blake's wife. I think you met him the night they brought me to the E.R."

"Oh, right." Isa moved to inspect the paint color and hoped he hadn't recognized any traces of jealousy in her tone at the mention of another woman helping him.

"Have you decided on a name for the café yet?"

Ethan shrugged. "I think I've just about decided. I want it to be the right name. I want it to mean something."

"It will come to you. So what's this?" she pointed to the floor-to-ceiling half wall in the center of the room.

"Fireplace. We're going to use real brick, but it will be a gas fireplace. Rachel says it will warm up the room, decoratively speaking."

"Good idea," Isa said, keeping her tone level. She knew Ethan wanted to share his excitement with her, but when it came to his new restaurant venture, she just wasn't feeling very excited.

"The wall over there will have artificial brick. I'm having hardwood floors laid early next week."

She bit back a grin. He looked like a kid on Christmas morning. She worked to stifle her attraction. It didn't help that on top of looking eager and adorable, Ethan also looked gorgeous. His blue T-shirt hugged him in all the right ways. His ratty khaki pants had paint splattered on them and there was sawdust in his hair—somehow it all made him even more appealing to her. She liked how he obviously intended to be hands-on with every aspect of his business.

Isa just looked at him, enjoying the chemistry that seemed to ignite every time she was near him, while at the same time trying to overlook it.

He must have realized she was staring at him. "I know I'm a mess," he said, dusting his pants.

She shrugged. "Messy looks good on you, Ethan."

He stepped closer to her, smiling as though he knew how he affected her.

"So you're saying you like me even when I'm a mess?"

Isa cleared her throat, thinking again of their kiss. "I guess I do. What can I say? I like messy."

"You like messy. I like chaos. Sounds like a good match to me." His eyes were bright, happy. "You can see that Rachel's going for a fire-station theme with her decorating. All the guys are donating some memorabilia. I think it's going to look pretty cool when we're finished. I'm still working on the new menu."

"Breakfast foods and then sandwiches and soups and salads, right?" Isa asked, wishing she didn't want to stand so close to him and feel him take her hand in his. She could only assume that it was her hesitancy that kept Ethan from being more forward with her. She knew he liked her. And she wanted him to like her. She just didn't want to do something crazy like fall head over heels in love, which she felt very much in danger of doing.

"Yeah and a couple of cheeseburgers. I'm thinking maybe a bacon-cheddar and a jalapeño-Jack."

"Sounds good."

"I could show you the menu once I've finished it," Ethan said, hope permeating his words.

Isa nodded, making sure she didn't come across as overly enthusiastic. "Sure, I'll take a look if you want me to."

"Would you like to see the kitchen?" Ethan stepped backward and Isa saw him flinch badly. She quickly reached for him and he gripped her arm.

"Ethan? What's wrong? Is it your back?"

He clenched his jaw, breathing hard.

"Okay, take a deep breath. Relax if you can. I'm right here—hold on to me."

He couldn't answer, but he took deep breaths as she instructed. Once some of the tension eased, Isa led him to a chair and helped him sit down. He sat with his back rigid, clearly in extreme pain.

"Did you go to therapy this morning?" she asked.

He shook his head. "Tomorrow," he told her. "I must have stepped wrong or something."

Isabella frowned. "Does it happen often?"

Ethan shrugged and Isa got the feeling he didn't want to tell her just how often he was experiencing that level of pain.

"When is your next doctor visit?"

"Not for a couple of weeks. For now I'm just supposed to be going to therapy. But it's brutal, Isabella. I feel like a wimp saying that to you. But I can't believe how hard therapy is."

"You're not a wimp, Ethan." Isabella shook her head. "You had a spinal fracture. You're hurting. It will get better. But talk to your doctor soon if you feel like something might be wrong. You need to be examined. And be sure to tell your therapist tomorrow about this incident. They might not want to work you so hard if you're still hurting this badly."

Ethan didn't answer and Isa knew he was still smarting. "What can I do, Ethan?" She knelt in front of him.

"A kiss might help," he said with a tiny smile.

Isa licked her lips and was reminded again of just how charming Ethan Carter could be.

"You know you're taking advantage of my concern for you, right?" Isa said.

Ethan just nodded. "Sometimes a guy has to do what a guy has to do."

Isa laughed. "The same goes for girls," she said before planting a soft kiss on his lips.

Isabella crept into the NICU after her shift the following Thursday morning, tiptoeing as nurses pointed at sleeping babies. She turned a corner and saw Maggie sitting in a rocking chair, her eyes closed.

"Mags?" Isabella whispered.

Her friend's eyes flew open. She relaxed once she saw it was only Isa.

"I must have dozed off," Maggie said, her voice just above a whisper.

Isa leaned down to hug her friend, then moved to the middle of the small space to look at Maggie's daughter, Bianca. The teeny-tiny baby girl lay sleeping in the incubator. She seemed so small to have so much equipment hooked up to her. Because her lungs hadn't fully developed, she was being given oxygen.

"Oh Maggie, she's beautiful," Isa said, touching the glass between herself and Bianca.

Maggie stood up and stretched. "I hate that she's in there. I feel like she needs to be held," Maggie said wistfully, tracing hearts on the glass.

Isa tucked her arm through her friend's. "You're right here loving her. Do they let you hold her at all?"

"A few times a day," Maggie said. She looked up at Isa. "Those are the highlights of every day for me."

Warm tears burned Isabella's eyes. She hugged Maggie.

"The important thing is that she's going to be fine."

"She's so little," Maggie countered.

"For now. She'll grow, Maggie. You know she will. She'll be playing soccer before you know it."

That drew a small smile from Maggie. "Let's walk down for a soda," she suggested, and Isa followed her through the NICU. They reached the hospital cafeteria and Isa ordered fries and two cans of Coke. Then the two girls found a bench outside to share.

"You look great, Maggie," Isa said, knowing how much encouragement her friend needed. But the words didn't help; Maggie looked at Isa with tears in her eyes.

"I feel like a disaster. I almost lost Bianca."

Isa had no doubt that Maggie's hormones were raging and that she was more than a little emotionally unsteady. She reached over and rubbed Maggie's hand, looking right into her eyes.

"Mags, that wasn't your fault. You couldn't have known about the cervical insufficiency. It was scary, and you're right, it could have been much worse. But Bianca was viable. She's here. She's going to be fine. You both will be."

"It could happen again if I try to have another baby."

Isa heard the trepidation in Maggie's words. She shook her head.

"Next time they'll watch you more closely. They'll know the risk. You're a nurse. You know there are measures to prevent preterm labor. Listen to me—right now you need to concentrate on yourself and on Bianca. You should keep taking your prenatal vitamins. And you need to keep your strength up. Are you nursing?"

Maggie shook her head. "She's so small that she really struggled to latch on. And I'm not producing very much milk. I'm pumping what I can. And we're supplementing with formula." Maggie's disheartened tone made Isa think this was another source of guilt for Maggie.

"You're already a *great* mother, Maggie," Isa said firmly. "I think Bianca is lucky to have you. You had no control over when Bianca was born. And you can't control how much milk you can produce. These things are not your fault. You've got to let go of these expectations."

"She's so little." The weepiness returned and Maggie started to cry. "I was so afraid."

Isa held Maggie's hand tightly.

"I was, too. If you need to talk through everything that happened, I'm here, Maggie. You can talk about whatever you want to. You can tell me exactly how you're feeling. I want to encourage you. I want you to know I'm here for you—anything I can do to help. I mean it when I say just ask. We're friends, Mags. You are never alone in this."

"I'm glad Ethan was there," Maggie said.

"Me too," Isa agreed.

"He's a good man, Isa."

"He is."

"I think you're a good team."

"Maybe," Isa allowed.

They were both quiet for a moment, and then Maggie drew in a shaky breath.

"They want me to go home tonight."

Isa could see the distress in Maggie's eyes at the thought of being away from her baby.

"Bianca will probably be here for at least four more weeks."

Isa didn't say anything for a moment. She could say it would be all right, but the truth was that her friend was going home and her baby was staying in the NICU. Isa wouldn't feel all right if it were her. Maggie's hand was cold. Isa scooted closer to her on the bench.

"You prayed for me in the car," Maggie said in a low voice.

Isa was surprised that Maggie even remembered.

"It was more like I yelled for you," Isa admitted, and

Maggie chuckled, then groaned and touched her stomach where her stitches were from the Cesarean section.

"Don't make me laugh, Isabella Romano." Maggie patted Isa's hand this time. "Yelling, praying—sometimes they are the same thing."

Isa looked down at her knees. "Do you really think so?"

"Yes."

"I was afraid God wouldn't help us."

Maggie nodded. "I was afraid of that, too."

"He's so unpredictable," Isa said, with a slight edge to her tone. But Maggie just looked out at the scene of mountains in the distance. The weather felt warm around them and the sky was picture-perfect clear; they could still see the mountaintops.

"He is. But I keep thanking Him for Bianca's life. I keep thanking Him that you were there, that Ethan was there, that Leo drove us to the hospital quickly and safely. I needed all of you, and God made sure you were there for me." Maggie drew in a ragged breath, full of emotion. "I'd nearly given up, Isa. Before I got pregnant with Bianca, I'd just about given up hope of ever being a mother. I thought I'd missed my chance."

"I know," Isa whispered.

"There were many times after my miscarriages when doubt filled my heart. But right now, with the knowledge that I'm a mother and my baby girl is alive and growing stronger every day, I know that God is a God of second chances. And third and fourth chances. He's that kind of God, Isa. Just when we think things won't work out…or certain dreams can't come true…God surprises us. Sometimes I feel so afraid when I see Bianca in that incubator. But at the same time, I feel so grateful that God gave her to me." Maggie turned to face Isa. "Isa, I need to tell you something. I don't plan to come back to work. Not anytime soon. Bianca's so small and she'll be in the hospital for such a long time—she needs me. José's going to look for a second job."

Isa masked the sinking of her heart with an upbeat nod. "Of course. I completely understand, Maggie. I would do the same thing."

Maggie turned back to face the mountains. "I'll miss you."

Isa could barely swallow from the lump in her throat. "You won't have to. We'll see each other all the time. You're practically a Romano."

Maggie gave her a small smile. "That's true. I should get back. Walk with me."

They walked side by side, with Isa trying not to think about the fact that Maggie wouldn't be working with her any longer.

"I'll be coming here every day until Bianca is discharged," Maggie told her.

"I'd expect nothing less. I'll come up as often as I can," Isa promised. They reached Bianca's incubator, and again Isabella marveled at the tiny baby. As Isa turned to leave, Maggie held her back for a moment.

"Isa, thank you. For being with me, for supporting me, for caring enough to pray on my behalf—thank you."

"You're my friend, Maggie. It's what friends do."

Maggie nodded. "You can do one more thing for me."

"Name it."

"Give that good-looking fireman a real chance."

The corners of Isa's lips turned upward at the very thought of that good-looking fireman.

Ethan.

Chapter 9

Ethan gritted his teeth. He'd spent the past hour doing exercises and receiving massage therapy at Incline Physical Therapy and Wellness Center.

You can do this. It's not so bad.

Ethan hated to admit it, but the personal pep talks weren't working.

"How are you doing, Ethan?" Keira, the physical-therapy assistant who nearly always worked with him during his sessions, asked.

"Okay," Ethan answered tightly, trying to push through the sting.

"Isaac said he wants you to do at least ten of these exercises before we cool down. Can you handle that?"

Ethan held back from voicing his feelings on whether he could handle the exercises. He knew Isaac and Keira were only trying to help him regain strength, but it felt like too much. By midexercise he couldn't hold it in. Ethan gasped from the pain in his back and froze.

"Okay. Breathe out. It's going to be okay, Ethan," Keira said calmly, easing him through the intense pain.

By the end of his session, Ethan felt the way he usually did—exhausted and frustrated with his lack of progress.

"We're going to go ahead and do some heat and stem treatment. That will feel a lot better, trust me," Keira told him. "You just need to relax and let the heat do the rest."

"Am I still on track? I don't really feel like I'm progressing like I should be," he finally said. He told her about the episode he'd experienced at the café the day before. Keira handed him a bottle of water.

"It's different for everyone, Ethan. You're anxious to have this behind you, but really, it's just got to follow its course. These things take time. Healing isn't always a fast process. You've got to understand and accept that. You've made progress. I know it feels like it takes forever, but it doesn't. It's only been a couple of weeks of therapy. The next time you come in, I'll have Isaac do an evaluation on how you're progressing."

Ethan drank half his bottle of water and didn't answer. It was true he'd hoped he'd be further along by this point. But how long was it going to take? He'd worn that back brace for six weeks. When the doctor cleared him to begin therapy, he'd felt so confident that surely he'd be back to normal soon. But he still felt so much pain; he still felt so unlike himself.

He thought of the strength he'd need to resume his duties as a firefighter. The thought dispirited him. He didn't feel anywhere close to being able to handle those duties yet, as much as he wanted to. He held on to Keira's words and tried to be positive.

Time. It's going to take longer than I thought. I have to be patient. I'll be back to normal eventually.

Late the following afternoon, Ethan watched as the new sign for the café was maneuvered above the entrance.

"More to the right!" he called out to the guys working for him. He loved the sign. Rachel had designed it with the fire station in mind—fire-engine-red with gold letters. The sign popped with color and vibrancy. He'd been surprised by how much he'd enjoyed the redecorating aspect of taking over Mick's business. The bookkeeping was another matter, but he was getting the hang of things. Mick had been gracious enough to share his knowledge with him. Ethan knew he'd run the business according to his own style, but knowing the ropes was essential. After interviewing a number of candidates, he'd decided on another cook, Mark, and three more part-time servers. The cash flow going out stressed him more than he'd anticipated, no doubt about that. All the building materials for redecorating, Rachel's fee, not to mention overhead, payroll, food—Ethan tried not to let the amounts consume and overwhelm him.

He clapped as the sign was finally hung. "Looks great, guys! Thanks!" He left them outside to finish and disappeared back into the dining room, which looked nearly finished.

"What do you think, Ethan?" Rachel asked as she hung a final canvas picture. He studied the picture. It was a huge magnified photo of the Company 51 fire truck with all the guys on board. Ethan had hired a photographer to take a few photos around the fire station. Now photos of boots, hats and gear, the interior of the station, the guys in motion, and more lined the walls of his café. Rachel even had a portion of a ladder hanging parallel to the ceiling. The café decor captured the warmth, camaraderie and excitement of a fire station, and to Ethan it now felt like home.

"Rachel, you've done an incredible job. This café looks better than I could have ever dreamed."

The dark wood floors flowed throughout the restaurant, the faux brick was striking, the photos were beautiful and the brick fireplace took the design to another level, artistically speaking. Ethan couldn't have been more pleased.

"When's the grand opening?" Rachel asked.

"I'm hoping we open the doors for customers in another week or so."

By six o'clock the workers had all gone home and Ethan was alone with his café and could begin the part of his job as restaurateur that he enjoyed the most—cooking.

A tap on the glass told him Isa had arrived. By the time he reached the door, she'd moved back to the edge of the sidewalk, her face tilted upward as she examined the new sign. He moved to stand beside her.

"What do you think?" he asked her.

"You didn't tell me you'd chosen a name," she noted, her eyes still focused upward.

"It just came to me all of a sudden. And it felt right. I wanted to surprise you, to surprise everyone."

She nodded. They both looked up, reading the sign silently together.

Second Chance Café.

"Well?" Ethan probed.

"I like it, Ethan. You're right. It fits."

With a smile, he draped an arm around her shoulders and steered her inside the building. Then he stood happily, soaking in her praise as she admired the dining room.

"So you said you needed my help? I hope food is involved because I'm starving," Isa said, and Ethan grinned.

"Follow me to the kitchen." He pushed through the swinging door and Isa inhaled deeply.

"What are you making?"

"We," he corrected her, "are making corn chowder. I really want to have it on the menu, but my recipe needs tweaking. It's good, but it needs to be more than good."

Isa nodded. "Where do you want me, Chef?"

Chef. He liked the sound of that. He tossed her an apron and pointed to a workstation on her left. "Bacon needs to be chopped and fried to a crisp, and potatoes need to be peeled."

"I'm on it."

They talked lightly as they cooked together, joking back and forth as usual. Ethan pulled two fruit pies out of the refrigerator and set them on the counter. Then he pulled a pan of roasted chicken and vegetables out of the oven, along with a broccoli-and-rice casserole.

"This is enough food for an army, Ethan. What are we doing with all of it?" Isa asked.

"We're packaging it up and taking it over to José and Maggie. They can freeze it and have ready-made meals."

Her mouth dropped open. She looked away after a moment. Ethan knew her well enough to assume that Isa was again trying to take control of her emotions. "That's a great idea," she said in a quiet voice.

Ethan walked over to her and put both hands on her shoulders. "Isa," he said, tilting her chin up to make eye contact. "It's okay, you know."

She went up on her tiptoes and kissed him. "Thank you." She pushed him back. "Now let me work. And by the way, your corn chowder recipe doesn't call for cheddar. That's a mistake. Cheese makes everything better."

He nodded. "Go for it. Make whatever changes you want."

Isa let herself unwind as Ethan gave her the space she needed to cook. He turned on some music while they both worked independently of each other. Isa washed her hands and studied his corn chowder recipe. She hated to admit it, but having a restaurant kitchen at her fingertips was rather fun. She'd spent years alongside her father and brother in the Romano's kitchen. But now she rarely ever cooked for pleasure for herself. Takeout and fast food had become common parts of her life due to her hectic schedule. She'd forgotten how much she loved cooking with fresh ingredients, taking the time to create something special, something meant to be shared.

For a moment, Isa was distracted. She thought of Ethan's chosen name for his café, the Second Chance Café. And she couldn't help thinking of Maggie's assertion that God was a God of second chances. And third chances and fourth and so on.

The thought comforted her for some reason.

Ethan had already set out a soup pot for her with a stack of ingredients on the counter, along with about six ears of corn. She heated olive oil and butter, adding onion and garlic. She rummaged through the refrigerator for heavy cream and cheddar and set them on the counter.

Once the soup was simmering, she wiped down the counters, enjoying the aroma of the chowder. Her stomach growled and she was pleased to see that Ethan had set out bread and bruschetta for them to munch on while they cooked.

"We haven't talked about it, you know," Ethan said.

Isa froze and an uncomfortable look crossed her face. "What haven't we talked about?"

"The fact that you seem to have resigned yourself to dating a chef," Ethan said lightly.

The clouds in her eyes scattered and Isa pressed her lips together to keep from letting him see her telltale smile.

"I told you, this is on a trial basis, tough guy," Isa rebuffed.

"Can I ask you something, Isa?" Ethan asked.

She sighed. "If you must."

"Would you go to church with me sometime?"

She stopped in her tracks and looked at him with interest. She watched him wait while she considered the question.

"Yes," she said finally.

"Yes?" he echoed.

She spooned a portion of the bruschetta onto a piece of toasted bread, appreciating the aroma of basil and olive oil, tomatoes and balsamic vinegar. She took a bite and let the flavors come together.

"This is excellent bruschetta, Ethan," she complimented him.

"I'm glad you like it. I figure if I'm going to date a Romano, I should perfect a few of my Italian dishes."

Isa laughed. "I could help you with that, you know."

He leaned over the large island in the kitchen, his gaze still full of fun but a little more serious. "Isabella Romano, I'll take cooking lessons from you anytime, anyplace. I'll do whatever it takes."

How did he *do* that? Get under her skin so easily? Isa stared at her bruschetta, feeling overcome by her pull to Ethan. It was as though he knew the way to reach her. He was verbal and playful and forward and self-confident— Isabella's own recipe for the perfect guy.

Except there were no perfect guys. She knew that for a fact.

"All right," he said, interrupting the silence. "So you're willing to go to my church? How about next Sunday?"

"Yes, I'm willing. And yes, I'll go next Sunday. The truth

is that I haven't gone to church in a while. Why do you want me to go with you?"

Ethan pretended to think over the subject. "So we can hold hands and text notes to each other."

She giggled, the sound filling the space between them.

"All kidding aside, Redeemer Community is a great church. Several of the firefighters go there when they're not on shift. I think you'll like it. And I'll like sitting beside you," Ethan said.

"So you're not really planning on holding hands, then?" Isabella said, shaking her head with mock disappointment.

"Oh, I'm totally planning on it," he replied with confidence.

Isa downed a second espresso only two hours into her shift that night. Being Friday, it was supposed to be her night off, but a friend had needed someone to cover for her because of a family emergency. So as usual, Isa had said yes.

I can't keep up this schedule. Working all night, going by Mom and Dad's whenever I can, seeing Ethan every time I have a free moment—I feel like I'm running out of gas. I haven't had a decent night's sleep since before Mandy had baby Tony. It's been one thing after another and I'm about to crash. I can feel it coming. But what am I supposed to change? I have to work—I've got bills to pay. We're short-staffed with Mags gone, so I have to pick up the slack. Mom and Dad mean everything to me, and I know Mom has more peace of mind when I stop by to check on Dad. Plus, I can see how Dad lights up when I come to see him.

I've been running up to the NICU a lot to see Maggie. But she needs all the support she can get. She's barely hanging by an emotional thread as it is. I try to check in

*with Mandy as much as possible because I want to be the
kind of sister-in-law who helps out when she's needed and
I know Mandy's adjusting to motherhood and needs help.*

*Daughter, sister, friend, nurse. Is there even room for
girlfriend to be added to that list?*

Her thoughts drifted to Ethan and the café and the
fun they'd had cooking together. Isabella loved that he'd
thought of making food for Maggie and José. Maggie had
cried when they'd shown up on her doorstep with sacks of
meals to freeze. Isabella thought about baby Bianca and
the fact that Maggie wouldn't be returning to the hospital, at least not for the foreseeable future. The thought of
working the night shift without Maggie was a bleak one.

With a sigh, Isabella stood up and made her rounds,
feeling exhausted and depressed about Maggie's resig-
nation.

She also worried about Ethan. The night they'd cooked
together, she'd noticed how gingerly he moved. The pain
in his back seemed sustained. Granted, he'd experienced
a bad fall, but still, she worried about whether he was
healing properly. He didn't seem to want to talk about it.
Being someone who didn't like it when others pried into
her life, she didn't want to press him if he didn't feel like
discussing it. But she couldn't help worrying. He winced
often without even realizing it.

By the time 6:00 a.m. rolled around, Isabella was running on fumes. Around 1:00 a.m. a bad car accident had
resulted in a crowd of people being rushed to the E.R. And
a case with a child's injuries had caused Isabella to involve
Child Services right before her shift ended. She trudged
through the hospital parking lot, taking a moment to lean
against the car and tilt her face up to the sunlight. But even
the Colorado sunshine couldn't revitalize her.

Still, she pulled together what energy she had left and

sent her mother a text before leaving to grab a drive-through breakfast sandwich. She then drove over to her parents' home, feeling a tad guilty she hadn't been around as much during the past few weeks. With Mandy's labor and delivery, and then Maggie's unexpected preterm labor and delivery, Isa felt as though she'd been living in a whirl-wind lately. A whirlwind that seemed to revolve around babies. She pulled into the driveway, shocked to see Leo's car. The sight sent alarm into her chest. She ran to the house and used her key to get in.

"Mom?" she called out. Her mother poked her head around the kitchen and put a finger to her lips. Isa lowered her voice, dropped her purse and rushed to the kitchen. Leo sat at the table drinking a cup of coffee.

"Isa, we were waiting for you. Dad's taking a nap," he said, motioning for her to sit next to him. She poured herself a cup of coffee and sat at the table. Her mother sat across from them.

"I called Leo this morning and asked him to come by after I received your text, Isabella," her mother explained. "I want to talk to both of you."

Isa felt her heart plummet. *Not more bad news. Please, God.*

"At your father's doctor appointment yesterday, Dr. Rosas recommended we consider brain surgery."

"Deep brain stimulation," Isa surmised, letting the notion sink in.

"After speaking with Dr. Rosas, I want Gabriel to have the surgery. She thinks he's a good candidate."

"I want to talk with her," Isa said.

"So do I," Leo echoed.

Their mother nodded. "I figured as much. We can schedule an appointment to speak with Dr. Rosas. Gabriel's symptoms are getting worse and the medications aren't helping as much. If surgery could help with the symptoms…well, I think it's worth a try."

"Does Dad want to do it?" Isa asked.

"Absolutely."

Isa and Leo exchanged a glance. She could see the hope in Leo's face.

"I'll call Dr. Rosas to schedule a meeting to discuss it, Mom," Isa said.

Once she got home, Isa pulled on her pajamas and hopped into bed, knowing her body needed rest. She tossed and turned, trying to get her thoughts to slow down. She finally woke after hours of restless sleep, thankful to have slept at all. Her mind couldn't seem to stop racing. The clock above the mantle told her it was after 5:00 p.m. She took a hot shower and then plugged in her laptop, determined to research brain stimulation for Parkinson's patients. An hour flew by as she read articles and surfed different medical sites. For the most part, she felt encouraged by what she'd read. The procedure wasn't too invasive and had a good success rate for helping Parkinson's patients. She knew that nothing short of divine healing would cure her father, but any relief for the symptoms would be welcome.

Isa felt the urge to pray for her dad, for the doctors, for wisdom all around. But she didn't quite know what to say. The inclination to pour out her heart before God startled her, and her immediate reaction was to hold back.

I don't want to be disappointed. With God, with relationships, with my dad's health, with everything—I keep battling disappointment.

She sat at her kitchen table, recognizing and acknowledging the underlying reason for her apprehension. A steady stream of disappointment had killed her hope.

Chapter 10

A bead of sweat fell to the table where Ethan was lying on his stomach the following Wednesday morning, receiving massage therapy after having finished the exercises lined up for him during their session.

"I'm guessing that hurts pretty badly, Ethan. Talk to me," Keira ordered.

"Yeah," he panted. "It's still hurting. The pain meds help, but I wish I didn't have to be so dependent on them just to get through the day."

Keira frowned. "Isaac is going to come take a look at you as soon as he finishes up with his current patient. I think we need to talk about your level of pain."

For the next half hour, Ethan was poked and prodded and examined by Isaac and Keira while answering questions as honestly as he could about his progress, or lack thereof. Before Ethan left, Isaac informed him he'd be speaking with Ethan's doctor soon about the appropriate next steps, which would include more testing.

He drove straight to the café afterward and eased out of the truck carefully. He stopped, holding on to the door for a moment.

God, I could really use Your help right now. I have a grand opening in days and I'm finding it hard to walk, stand, sit, not to mention cook.

With difficulty, Ethan spent the next two hours training his cooks on the new menu. He sat down as much as possible. He ended the session early and reached for his phone, wanting to hear Isabella's voice.

"Ethan?" Isa answered. "Everything okay?"

He gritted his teeth. "Yeah, I'm all right. My back is sore today."

"I'm sorry to hear that. I'm at the hospital right now. We're about to meet with my father's doctors."

"Has something happened?" His heart felt as though it had plunged to his stomach.

"No, we're just looking at options. I have to go."

"Oh. Would you…? Do you want me to come over there? Is there anything I can do?"

"No, it's a family thing. I can call you later."

Ethan stared at the phone after Isa had hung up, the hurt from his back now spreading to his heart. He picked himself back up and decided to call Caleb. He might as well box up all the leftover food from the cooking sessions and send it over to the guys next door. He'd rather eat with the firefighters than have to go home to his empty studio.

Isa folded her arms and looked from her mother to Leo.

"I'm for it," Leo said with conviction. "It could help. There are risks, yes, but right now Dad's unhappier than ever with his condition. He needs relief from the symptoms. I know it's not a cure. But it could *help*."

"He wants to do it, Isabella," her mother said.

Isa squeezed the bridge of her nose, wishing she knew what the outcome would be, wishing she knew the best course of action for her dad, for herself, for her family. "I know he does."

"So are we in agreement, then?" Leo asked. "Do we move forward with the surgery?"

The three of them stood in Dr. Rosas's office. After a lengthy consultation with the doctor, Isa, Leo and her mother were discussing the situation while Gabriel began a few tests. Isa paced the room. She stopped after a moment.

"I vote yes. If Dad wants the surgery, I vote yes. I'm very comfortable with Dr. Rosas, and she'll be working closely with the neurology center every step of the way," Isa yielded.

Her mother took a deep breath, her eyes lighting with an optimism that worried Isa.

"Mom, you heard the risks. And you know Dad will still have Parkinson's. You understand that, right?"

Her mother nodded. "Of course I do. But if this surgery might improve his quality of life, it's a chance I want for him."

"All right, then. We'll tell Dr. Rosas we want to do all the necessary tests to make sure Dad's a good candidate for the surgery," Isa said.

Her mom reached out for both Isa and Leo to take her hands.

"Let's pray together."

Isa closed her eyes and hoped God was listening.

Four days later Isa stood outside Redeemer Community Church, staring up at the large building.

"You made it!"

She turned to see a beaming Ethan walking up behind her.

"I told you I'd be here." He walked up to her and Isa's first thought was again of how *tall* Ethan was. Sometimes she felt as if he towered over her. She reminded herself to wear heels the next time they were together. Looking up at him, she was also reminded of how handsome he was. In just dark jeans and a shirt with the fire-station logo, he still made her heart rate accelerate. She tilted her head to the side, enjoying the view of Ethan.

"I know," he said. "But I also know you worked the late shift last night unexpectedly. I wasn't sure you'd have the energy to stay up."

Isa held up a Grande-sized Starbucks cup. "I'm fueled for the moment. Just nudge me if I start to snore or something. I hate to turn down extra shifts. The additional money always helps."

He led her into the church, assertively taking her hand in his. She liked the big open sanctuary and the easy friendliness of the churchgoers. Many knew Ethan and stopped to say hello to both of them. She knew they looked like a couple, walking around holding hands, standing so close to each other.

They sat together and Isa liked the fact that Ethan never let go of her hand. She couldn't deny that he was beginning to feel more like a boyfriend than just a guy she casually dated. Even to her they seemed like a couple.

He brings me chocolate-stuffed croissants for breakfast. When he kisses me, I'm almost sure I'm in love.

His blue eyes make me lose my train of thought at any given moment.

The list could go on. She chose not to think about it. Isa knew from experience that chemistry could happen with any number of guys. She needed more than chemistry.

She needed longevity.

The worship team began to sing and Isa tried to relax.

She wasn't sure why she felt so uneasy. For goodness' sake, she'd been attending church for nearly as long as she'd been alive. Why, then, did she feel uneasy? She considered that it had been probably six months since she'd darkened the door of the church she normally attended with her parents.

It's just been a while. I feel like something of a stranger to church, I guess.

The song leader paused between songs. He sat perched on a stool near the podium and smiled out at the congregation.

"Do you ever feel like you need a new song?"

Isa sat unmoving in her seat.

"I'm not just talking about a new worship song for us to learn. I'm talking about a new song in your heart. Have you ever felt completely dry, maybe discontent? Like you need something new, something fresh? You want to feel alive. You need a new song to well up inside you. But have you ever felt like you couldn't find that song on your own? I have felt that way. Psalm 40:3 tells us that God can put a new song in our mouths and that many will see it and fear and trust in the Lord. Maybe you're thinking that you can barely trust in God yourself, so no one is going to look at you and learn to trust in God."

Isa stared down at her hands, blinking rapidly to hold back any wayward waterworks. But the room was quiet and she had to peek back up at the song leader. He had a knowing smile, a peaceful look in his eyes.

"You'd be surprised by what God can do."

Isa tried to concentrate on flipping through the church newsletter she'd received upon entering the sanctuary. She hoped the worship part of the service would end quickly.

"For those of us feeling dry...I want to remind us all that Christ came that we might live abundantly. Dry and discontent are not your future. Don't believe that. A new song is waiting to fill your heart."

Even with her head down, her eyes glued to the newsletter, Isa had to struggle for breath. She thought of her dad. Even trapped in a body that wouldn't let him do the things he wanted to do, he seemed more at peace than she felt.

The thought shamed her.

I don't want to be here, she told herself, though the words didn't quite ring true with her heart. She didn't like the guilty feelings that always seemed to accompany going to church. But something in her didn't want to leave. Her soul felt parched.

A new song. A more abundant life. Dry and discontent.

Every word pricked her heart.

She glanced over at Ethan, prepared to whisper to him that she was feeling exhausted and needed to leave. But his eyes were on her, watching her seriously.

"You're right where you need to be, Isa. Trust me," he whispered in a low voice. She looked into those intense blue eyes. His hand tightened around hers and the ensnared sensation she'd felt wrap around her like a rope just moments before seemed to lessen as a result of the gentle pressure of Ethan's strong hand.

Isa exhaled.

A new song.

I wish.

"Do you think you'd like to go again with me next week?" Ethan asked as they walked through the church parking lot together. He was unsure as to how Isa might respond.

She fiddled with the keys in her hand. "I'll have to see."

He just nodded. "Of course. It's an open invitation, Isa."

She stopped by her car. "I liked your church, Ethan. Really, I did."

"It could be your church, too."

She looked past him at the parking lot. "I should probably go home and sleep for a while."

"Or," Ethan began, "you could have lunch downtown with me. Your choice."

She smiled Ethan's favorite smile, the one filled with amusement and interest.

"My choice? Well, I'm not going to pass that up. Hop in my car and I'll drive. I owe you a family dinner, Ethan."

He didn't even try to conceal his surprise. "Dinner with your family?"

"That's right. We're eating at Romano's today. The family's gathering in one of the banquet rooms at the Franklin Street location. Interested?"

Interested in being part of a real family dinner? Interested in Isa actually including him in a special family gathering? Interested in being with people rather than being alone?

He cleared his throat, trying to control his eagerness. "That sounds great, Isa. Thank you for inviting me."

"No problem. You invited me first anyway. And I owe you a family dinner after how the last one you attended went."

"To be fair, you warned me there'd be commotion," Ethan said with a shrug.

Isa laughed. "True. But we don't normally have women going into labor!"

Twenty minutes later Ethan followed Isa through the large Romano's restaurant until they reached a spacious room, closed off, in the back. The room was bursting at the seams with people. Ethan recognized many from the short time he'd spent at Isa's parents' home the day Maggie had gone into labor. A buffet table lined the back wall and the smells of warm Italian dishes drifted through the room.

"Take Tony," Mandy instructed. Isa's sister-in-law walked up to Ethan and Isa. She grinned at Ethan.

"Ethan! So nice to see you," Mandy said as she passed the baby to Isa. "I'm starving and Leo disappeared into the kitchen. They're a bit short-staffed, so he'll probably have to work. Grab a seat for me by you guys, would you?"

Ethan noticed that Isa looked thrilled to take the baby; she patted Tony's back and whispered to him softly as Mandy joined the buffet line.

"Go make your plate, Ethan. I'll find seats for us and Mandy," Isa instructed.

Once his plate was nearly overflowing with lasagna, salad, chicken parmesan and mushroom ravioli, Ethan found Isa near the head of the table. She passed Tony to her mother while she went to the buffet. Left sandwiched between Isa's mother and her sister-in-law, he tried to keep up with the myriad conversations around him. Isa's mother often spoke in Italian to certain family members.

"It's okay, Ethan," Mandy said with a light smile. "You'll get used to it. Leo sometimes rattles off to me in Italian and I don't understand one word."

Ethan shrugged, "I don't mind. It must be nice to be part of such a large family."

She looked at him thoughtfully. "Isa mentioned that you're…well, not so used to a large family."

He finished a bite of lasagna and wiped his mouth. "The firefighters of Company 51 are my family. But other than that—no, I don't really have a family."

He appreciated that she didn't make a big deal out of it.

"You know what I think?" she said in a low voice.

He leaned close to hear her amid the noise.

"Families come in all shapes and sizes. The people in

this room make up one of the most loving, beautiful families that I've ever seen. Not perfect, but they're a picture of what I think family ought to be. They can make each other crazy, but they love each other like nothing I've ever seen before. The Romanos are special, Ethan. And if Isa brought you to family dinner today, she thinks you're pretty special, too."

He smiled at her, grateful for her words.

"She's hard to read sometimes, you know?" Ethan said regarding Isabella.

Mandy laughed. "She's a challenge. I'm guessing that's part of why you like her."

Ethan looked over at Isa by the buffet table. She stood with her hands on her hips, arguing with someone he was fairly certain was her cousin; the two girls looked so similar. Within seconds both girls were laughing and Isa's bright smile lit up the corner of the room. She shook back her dark hair and Ethan was again taken aback by how beautiful she was.

He knew in that instant that he'd been waiting for a woman like Isabella Romano for a long time without even knowing it. For so long he hadn't even been interested in dating. Work was his life. Fighting fires gave him fulfillment. He'd dated now and then—all the wives of his friends tended to try to set him up with their single girlfriends. But dating had always felt casual, and he'd intentionally kept it that way. But now…he wanted more. Maybe he'd wanted more for even longer than he realized.

And he wanted it with Isabella.

Her family just happened to be a bonus.

"Ethan," Mandy said, interrupting his thoughts. He glanced over at her. "When I say Isa's a challenge, I mean it. If you want to win her heart, you'll have to dive in for the long haul. She'll need proof."

"Proof?" he echoed.

Mandy nodded without further explanation. Isa's mother passed Tony back to Mandy and Isa joined them at that moment, breathless with laughter. She sat down between Mandy and Ethan.

"What were you two talking about?" Isa whispered to Ethan.

He shrugged. "You."

She smiled as though she didn't mind.

"I want to remind you that you *did* say you were looking for more chaos in your life, remember?" Isa teased.

Ethan winked at her, leaning closer until Isa held her breath.

"I'm pretty sure I found the chaos I was looking for, Isabella." He whispered the words so only she could hear them. He could see her weighing his words, unable to find her own. He enjoyed the blush rising in her cheeks.

"Did you just associate me with pandemonium, Ethan Carter?" she whispered back.

"You said it, Isabella Romano," Ethan answered with a grin.

Chapter 11

Ethan wiped the sweat from his brow. Five-fifteen in the morning and he was already stressed beyond belief. In just two hours, the Second Chance Café would open. *His* café would open. He'd spent the past week at the café day and night, preparing to open. Every day, his cooks had prepared a trial service in order for Ethan to ensure that the food was up to par. Bread was baking, the new menus were ready to be handed out, the casual, firefighter-style T-shirts for the waitstaff had arrived, the sign out front looked inviting and beautiful—all that was needed was paying customers.

It's now or never.

Ethan pulled pans of bread from the ovens. He'd arrived to begin baking bread at 3:00 a.m., along with a second baker. The kitchen, drenched with the scent of fresh, hot homemade bread, smelled incredible. By 6:00 a.m., both cooks had arrived and they were prepping for a breakfast rush. The firefighters had helped spread the word for the past several weeks, passing out flyers all over the city in anticipation of the grand opening of the Second Chance Café. Blake's college-aged son had created an amazing website for Ethan. With a few finishing touches, Rachel had the interior dining room ready and it was striking. The gas fireplace indeed made the dining room inviting and attractive.

Ethan could barely breathe from nervousness. He'd be cooking for strangers, people there to critique his culinary creations.

What if no one showed?

He felt sick.

Oh, God, I didn't expect to feel so nervous. What if I fail? What if this whole enterprise was just plain crazy on my part? What if no one likes the food? What if I don't make any money?

Ethan took a deep breath. He'd been trying to memorize Scripture ever since he'd accepted Christ—one of Caleb's suggestions.

He stepped outside the kitchen into the dining room for a moment alone. He placed both hands on the coffee bar and bowed his head.

When I am afraid, I will trust in you. The Bible verse flooded his heart. It was a simple, short verse, and one of the first he'd memorized. He held on to it for dear life.

When I am afraid, I will trust in you.

"Ethan?"

He opened his eyes to the sight of one of the waitresses studying him. "I checked the bathrooms—everything looks fine. I made sure all the silverware has been rolled up. The guys in the back said that the kitchen is prepped. We're ready."

He nodded at her, again wiping the sweat from his forehead. "It's five till seven. I'm going to go ahead and open up." Ethan unlocked the front doors. A smile crossed his face at the sight of the fire chief standing at the door.

"Chief Rawlins!"

"I wanted to be your first customer, Carter."

Ethan swallowed the boulder in his throat and held the door open. "Welcome." Ethan stepped aside as Jenny, his head waitress, led Chief Rawlins to the coffee bar and poured him a cup of coffee while he perused the menu. The front doors opened and a host of rowdy firefighters clambered inside. Ethan grinned as he disappeared into the kitchen to start working. The orders were steady. Ethan had expected a busy first day with the excitement of a new café, and he was not disappointed.

Jenny poked her head in the kitchen at about seven-thirty. "We've got a customer who wanted to compliment your *pain au chocolat*."

Ethan couldn't stop the smile from coming to his face. "About five foot four? Dark hair and dark eyes?"

Jenny laughed as she went back to the dining room.

Ethan washed his hands and checked the status of all the orders before stepping out behind the coffee bar. There sat Isa at the bar, the most beautiful woman for miles. He waved as Mick and Kay walked through the door, holding up one finger for Isa to give him a moment. He walked over to the older couple.

"Mick! Kay! What do you think of our café?"

Mick patted him on the back proudly. "It's all yours, Ethan. And we're proud of you."

"Oh, Ethan!" Miss Kay exclaimed. "It looks wonderful. Congratulations. We both wanted to be here to let you know we support you one hundred percent. I can't tell you how thrilled I am to see you take over this place. It was time for a new generation to step in."

"How are the Alaska plans coming along?" Ethan asked.

"Change of plan. We're heading to Kenya! We want to experience an African safari!" Miss Kay's smile was ear to ear. Ethan thanked them both for coming and then headed back to the coffee bar as they were seated.

"Hi, Chef. Congratulations on your grand opening!" Isa said. She sipped a cappuccino. "Looks like a good turnout to me," she commented, scanning the room filled with customers.

"Well, you know how it goes. It's a novelty today. We'll see how it looks tomorrow."

She smiled. "I *do* know how it goes. Good food brings people back, Ethan. And you've got that. I just finished your blueberry pancakes with sausage and sunny-side up eggs. I can promise you I'll be a repeat customer."

"Thank you for that, Isa."

"So did I just hear you say the blueberry pancakes are stellar?"

Isa turned around with a smile as Leo and Mandy joined her at the bar. Ethan blinked in surprise.

"Thanks so much for coming! Where's Tony?" he asked.

Leo rolled his eyes. "My mother thinks that if she doesn't get to watch him at least once a day, we're depriving her."

Isa laughed and hugged Mandy. "Yes, the blueberry pancakes are great. But I almost ordered the banana waffles with hashbrowns and bacon. You better check the menu, sis."

"I need to get back to the kitchen," Ethan said almost apologetically, still moved that Isa's family had come to his grand opening. But Leo waved him away.

"Go. We understand, Ethan. Run your kitchen."

The door swung behind Ethan as he left the dining room and Isa turned her attention back to her cappuccino.

"You didn't tell me you were coming," she said to Leo. He shrugged.

"We wanted to show up for your boyfriend's big day, Isa. That shouldn't surprise you."

"He's not my—"

"Isa," Leo and Mandy said together.

She chuckled. "Fine. Call him whatever you want."

"How's his back doing?" Mandy asked, exchanging a glance with Isa. She'd noticed it, too, then. Ethan's tendency to move cautiously, the flinch he made at times, the signs that he was in pain.

"I'm not sure. He says therapy is going slowly. I know it's been a difficult healing process."

"I hope he's not overdoing it with all this cooking. He'll be on his feet for hours," Leo noted. Isa didn't answer. The same thought troubled her. "He probably doesn't realize how all-consuming restaurant ownership is," Leo continued.

Mandy poked his shoulder but Isa just swallowed hard, knowing Leo could be right. Her reservations about dating someone with a restaurant started to resurface.

"It's a café, Isa. I think he'll have more flexibility," Mandy said.

I doubt it.

"It's not just his flexibility, Isa. Don't blame Ethan," Leo said, inspecting the menu. "How's your schedule at the moment?"

Isa just shook her head. "Don't ask. Especially with Maggie's absence at the E.R., I'm taking on more shifts. Then I've got Dad to think of. Plus, I keep trying to run up to the NICU to see Maggie and Bianca as often as possible. Then there's Tony—"

"Don't drag your nephew into this. He's an infant!" Leo argued.

"*Puh-lease.* He adores me and I refuse to neglect my relationship with him."

Mandy chuckled. "You do have a lot going on, Isa. Something's got to give, sweetheart."

Leo flipped over the menu to look at the lunch section. "Hey! Did you see this?"

Under Soups, Isa read the words *Isabella's Cheddar Corn Chowder.* The corners of her mouth turned up inadvertently.

"Since when are you an expert on corn chowder?" Leo teased.

Isa swatted his hand. "I have skills you know not of. But really, I just made a few tweaks to his recipe. It needed cheese."

"And he named it after you. That was sweet, Isa," Mandy said.

It really was. He's sweet. And gorgeous. And kind. And a dedicated believer. And a restaurant owner. And someone who wants more from me than I might be able to give. He's someone who could break my heart.

What am I so afraid of? Isa sighed, frustrated with her own mixed emotions. *Isn't this what I've wanted? Some great guy to drop into my life and spin me on a whirlwind romance? Ethan is the kind of guy I've always looked for. Why would I hold back now?*

Why do I feel like I'm still waiting for someone else?

Friday morning Isa pulled into the South Denver Neurology Center parking lot, quickly finding a spot and walking to the entrance, where Leo was waiting for her. He held out a Starbucks cup and she accepted it gratefully.

"Mom and Dad are already inside. They'll begin the tests in about twenty minutes. I'm glad you could make it," Leo said, pushing the door open for her. Isa stifled a yawn.

"Of course. How are Mandy and the baby?"

Leo didn't even try to stifle his yawn. "We're all exhausted. Tony was up every hour last night."

Isa squeezed her brother's side sympathetically. They joined their parents in the examination room for the consultation. After myriad tests, it now appeared that the deep brain stimulation surgery was a practical option for Isabella's father. They listened to the instructions on the necessary preparations prior to surgery and agreed that they would all return the following Thursday for her father's operation.

Isa clasped her hands together as she sat next to Leo.

Oh, God. I hope this is the best thing for Dad. Please let this help him.

Leo left to go to his office at the Franklin Street restaurant after the meeting, and Isa shooed him off, knowing he had payroll to take care of and that he was scheduled to cook for the Fifteenth Street location that evening. She drove her parents home, where she helped get her father settled and spent time processing the upcoming surgery with both of them. Talking about it seemed to help them with their decision, so Isa gladly sat and talked through everything she could with both of them. But by one o'clock she could barely keep her eyes open. Instead of driving home, she just fell onto the bed in her parents' guest room and shut her eyes.

She woke up after seven, stiff and unhappy at the thought that she'd have to go to work soon. She rolled over and looked out the window, light still streaming in. She loved the longer days of summer. It was the long nights that felt as though they were killing her. She pushed work out of her mind; going to the hospital was the last thing she wanted to do.

Isa wondered about Ethan. Other than texting back and

forth during the past few days, she hadn't seen him or talked to him since the café's grand opening. She knew he was glued to the restaurant right now, and she truly understood. He needed the café to be a success. And in reality, she didn't have any more free time than he did. She couldn't fault him for being so busy. She did, however, worry about whether he was overdoing it with his injuries.

She sighed and decided to call him. He answered by the second ring.

"Isa! I've missed you." His warm, immediate greeting filled her heart.

He's so open. He's so willing.

"How's the café?"

"It's been a really good first week. I think I'm gaining some regulars. And not just the guys next door."

"I hope you're not doing all the cooking, Ethan. You can't be on your feet that much while you're doing therapy. Your body needs rest."

"I know. I'm trying to delegate. But I'm cooking as much as I can. I love it, Isa."

Her chest tightened at the honesty in that statement. He sounded so happy. How in the world had she ended up interested in a guy who owned a restaurant? Hadn't she said a million times that she'd never get involved with someone in the restaurant business? Yet here she was, dating a fireman who doubled as a chef.

"The corn chowder seems to be a favorite," he told her.

Isa smiled. "Excellent." She gave him a quick rundown of her dad's doctor visit and explained that he'd be having surgery within the next couple of weeks.

"Can I help in any way? Really, Isa, I'm here for you. Anything. All you have to do is ask."

"I know," she answered. "Thanks, I'll let you know. But I know you're busy right now."

"I'm not too busy for you." His voice was so firm he sounded bothered.

"It's okay that you've got a full schedule, Ethan. So do I," Isa said, matching his firm tone. "You can't act like you've got all the free time in the world when you just started your own business."

"I'm not—I'm just…" She could hear Ethan inhale. "I'm just saying that I have time for you. I'll make time for you."

Isa didn't answer. The fact that he was already trying to reassure her that he could fit her into his life amid his restaurant duties rubbed her the wrong way. For as long as she could remember, her father and brother had done the same thing. She tried to shake off the annoyance. She knew Ethan was trying.

"I know you will. But we can only do so much with our schedules. I've got a lot going on right now, too."

"I know. But there's got to be a way for us to do this. Lots of people lead busy lives and still have time for a relationship."

There's that optimism of his, Isa thought. She mustered the ability to end on a mostly positive note before hanging up. She'd sensed they were on the verge of an argument and she just didn't have the energy for it. She needed to take herself home to get ready for work.

She walked through the nearly empty E.R. that night knowing that she was really too tired to be on the schedule. Her exhaustion resulted in her being snippy and easily frustrated with her colleagues. During her break, she ran up to the NICU to check on Bianca, hoping some time with the precious baby might help steady her temper. Maggie had told Isa that Bianca would be released from the hospital soon. Isa relaxed and spent a few moments rocking Bianca, who'd just had a feeding.

Isa stared down at the teeny baby. She seemed so small

compared to Leo's strong eight-pound-thirteen-ounce baby Tony. Bianca felt delicate and breakable. Isa breathed in the smell of her, dreaming of what it might be like to hold her own baby one day.

Small or large, healthy or frail, girl or boy—it must be the most marvelous feeling in the world to hold your own little one in your arms. To know he or she belongs to you. To know that you're his or her mother, to feel that intense love engulf you.

Isa didn't want to pray, but she couldn't seem to avoid it. The words just drifted from her heart.

God, you know my heart's desire for a family. You know how much I'd love to have a baby of my own and a hus-band of my own. Please...

But as she walked back down to the E.R. in the stillness of the night, her hands stuck in her pockets, Isa thought of her ever-growing list of obligations and responsibilities.

I can barely hold my head above water now—how could I add mother and wife to that list?

How could I not if I finally met the right guy? Those things have been wishes in my heart for so long. Now here comes Ethan, saying all the right things, doing all the right things—but how do I know? And why does this great guy finally show up right in the middle of all my disarray? I'm so unsure of everything. I'm so unsure of me. I'm so unsure of You.

She shook back her hair, feeling quiet and lonely and drained. She wanted to go home and crawl into bed and actually wake up feeling rested. She wanted to lie down and have her mind stop sprinting. Alone in the elevator, waiting to reach the E.R., a verse inundated her thoughts.

I am come that they might have life, and that they might have it more abundantly.

The words sounded like a whispered promise. But

promises eluded Isa. To her, life felt like an overly crowded schedule—too full, too much. Peace and relief seemed just a little out of reach. And an abundant life? At this point, Isa couldn't even picture it.

Chapter 12

The following Thursday morning, Ethan walked down the corridor of the South Denver Neurology Center in search of the waiting room. Isa sat up straight when she saw him enter the room and a look of relief covered her face. Ethan couldn't help wondering when she'd realize that she could count on him. He wanted her to expect him to show up for her. She always seemed so surprised by his presence, by his pursuit of her. She jumped up and took the eco-friendly bag from his hands.

"Tell me you brought me chocolate," she said, looking through the bag. He grinned.

"Hello to you, too. And you know I brought you chocolate. The stuffed croissants are somewhere in the bottom. There are some bagels and cheese Danishes, as well. How's your dad?"

"In surgery. No word yet. What are you even doing here? You have to be at the café!" Isa said, handing the bag to her mother, who joined them and gave Ethan a hug.

"I know. I need to get back. But I wanted you to know that I'm here, and that I'm praying for you."

Isa curled into him. She felt small and fragile in his arms, though he knew her to be one of the toughest women he'd ever met. He liked the combination. Their last conversation had perturbed him. Isa never seemed to have the confidence that he was available to her.

Is she available to you yet? He mulled the thought as Isa rested her head on his chest. *Sometimes.*

She's right. Ethan felt discouraged. *Neither of us is that available.*

Over the top of Isa's head, he saw her mother watching them, a surprised smile on her face.

He left the hospital, with Isa assuring him she'd keep him posted on her dad's progress. He rushed back to the café and took over in the kitchen, both slightly overwhelmed and thrilled to see the kitchen humming and orders coming through. The café was holding its own. The public's curiosity might have waned a bit since the grand opening, but he'd maintained a steady stream of customers. He'd been right in his assumption that the location was ideal and the café just needed some tender loving care.

He slid into his role as chef, savoring the experience of cooking for his own restaurant. It still shocked him how much he enjoyed owning a café. If it weren't for the nearly constant ache in his back, Ethan would have wondered if cooking was his second calling. As much as he loved fighting fires, the pleasure of running his own kitchen was a close rival.

As Ethan grilled cheeseburgers and plated sandwiches, he thought of how easily he'd adapted to life as a firefighter. The heavy gear, the substantial weight of responsibility that had come with the job—all of it had suited him like a favorite jacket. It had just fit, as though he'd been meant to be a firefighter all along. And yet running his kitchen felt just as natural, just as thrilling and just as satisfying.

Could he really do both? The twinge in his back as he stirred a huge pot of broccoli cheese soup made him doubt whether he could do either very well. By midafternoon Ethan let his assistant cook take over and he sat down in his office for a break. A short text from Isa had reassured him that her father had come through the surgery, and so far things looked positive. He held on to that good news as he made his way to Incline Physical Therapy and Wellness Center at five that evening.

"Keira," he said once they'd worked through a number of exercises, "I don't think I've improved very much over the last couple of weeks."

"I know it's slowgoing, and really, after nearly six weeks of therapy, you should be farther along. Isaac spoke with your doctor and we're recommending an MRI. At this point, we need to see if anything was overlooked in the X-ray. Your pain level is a definite concern. The meds won't maintain the same level of effectiveness as your body adapts to them. But don't forget that you've just taken on a whole new level of stress, Ethan. Right at the time when you should be healing and taking it easy, you've decided to become a business owner."

"I know," he admitted. "But I'm trying not to take on more than I have to. I'm not doing all the cooking. I'm not lifting. I'm trying to get the rest I need."

Keira put a pillow under his knees as he began his heat and stem therapy. "The MRI is necessary. And it should be done right away. Someone will be contacting you soon to set that up. After the MRI, we'll know where we are with therapy and what you need to move forward."

He nodded absentmindedly, his thoughts now on the

restaurant, the money he'd invested into this new venture, the fact that it would probably take months before he saw a profit, if then. The stress started to inch its way all through him.

God, I hope I've done the right thing. What if things never go back to the way they were before the accident? What if I'm always hurting? What if my life is permanently limited by this?

This time, Ethan couldn't talk himself out of feeling overcome by his situation.

Isa flipped through the channels, even though the TV was muted, in her dad's recovery room. Leo had just left to drive their mother home. They had decided that Isa would stay overnight. She knew Leo needed to go home to Mandy and Tony. And she didn't mind. It was her night off anyway, and she would rather be on a cot in her father's hospital room than anywhere else. She wanted to be there if he woke up and needed anything.

Dr. Rosas had smiled as she told them that Gabriel Romano had come through the first half of the surgery fine. All looked well. He'd go home the next day and come back a week later for part two of the deep brain stimulation. Even Isa's uncle, her father's brother, and aunt had flown in from Los Angeles to be with the family during the surgery. So Isa's mother had a houseful of guests. Isa slept intermittently, waking when nurses came in to check her dad. By morning she was relieved to see her dad responding so well. She knew they'd have to wait to see the results of the second half of the surgery, but so far she was encouraged. She sat with him while they waited for Leo and her mother to finish paperwork.

"How do you feel, Dad?" Isa asked, taking his hand in hers.

"I'm not sure really, Isa. All right, I guess. I'm afraid to think I feel better."

She noticed that he wasn't shaking quite as much and his words seemed to come just a little easier.

"I understand feeling that way. It can be scary to hope sometimes."

He looked at her and she felt as though her father could see all the way into her heart.

"I'm hoping for you, Isabella."

The immediate catch in her throat was followed by unstoppable tears rushing to her eyes. "For me? I'm talking about you, Dad."

He nodded, with still a small tremor. "I know you are, daughter. And you're very right—it can be a fearful thing to keep hoping. But sometimes, when you're afraid to even hope for good things, you just might need your father to hope for you. And I will never stop hoping for good things for my Isabella."

The words he spoke were clearer than she'd heard come from him in months—that alone would have been reason enough for Isabella to cry. And this time, Isa didn't even try not to.

Three days later Isa drove to Redeemer Community Church. She was still in the parking lot when she received a text from Ethan:

Not feeling great this morning. I'm not going to make it to church. Tell me how it goes.

She sat in the car for five minutes trying to decide whether to go in alone or not. Finally she got out, feeling guilty for wanting to leave without Ethan there by her side.

I drove here to go to church. I'm a grown woman who

*can go in by herself...and I can leave if I feel awkward.
I'll just sit in the back.*

She found a seat in the back row and felt semicomfort-
able until someone waved at her from across the aisle. She
recognized the guy as one of Ethan's firefighter buddies.

Oh great. Now he's walking over here.

She pasted on a smile as Caleb and a woman Isa assumed was his wife slid into the row next to her.

"Hi, Isabella!" Caleb said, and introduced her to his
wife, Hallie.

As they chitchatted, Isa felt less awkward. Worship
began and she let herself enjoy the music, conceding the
fact that she wanted to be there, that sitting with two people who wanted to be her friends was actually nice, and
that maybe, just maybe, being at church helped a little with
that thirsty feeling inside her.

After the service she talked with Caleb and Hallie, who
introduced her to a few more people at the church, and
then she decided to surprise Ethan. She picked up lunch
to go from a nearby deli and knocked on his door. When
the door opened, Isa did a double take. Ethan stood leaning against the doorway barefoot, wearing sweatpants and
a shirt that probably needed to be washed. His bloodshot
eyes told her he was exhausted.

"Are you okay?" she asked as he let her in. She depos-
ited the lunch sack on the kitchen counter and helped him
to the sofa.

"Yeah. Rough night. I may have worked too long in
the kitchen yesterday and I was really feeling it all night.
I didn't sleep well."

Isa stood in front of him, her hands on her hips. "This
is crazy. You're hurt. You shouldn't even be working yet
and you're trying to run a kitchen!"

He glared at her. "It was one bad day, Isa."

"It's a million bad days and you know it!" She raised her voice.

"Exaggerate much? I know I'm hurting. I'm getting an MRI soon."

"Why are you pushing yourself to the absolute limit? For what? To prove what?"

"I'm not proving anything! I bought a restaurant! I have to run it!" Ethan raised his voice to match hers.

"What were you thinking? Why did you do this?" Isa was yelling now. His anger only fueled her own.

"I was thinking that I didn't want to sit around and do nothing for months. I was thinking that I'd try something new. I was thinking it sounded like a great opportunity! I was thinking that I needed something to fall back on if I never get to be a firefighter again!" Ethan practically threw the words out at her.

Isa's blood pressure skyrocketed. "Here's a crazy thought. You might actually get well if you would let your body heal instead of taking on a new business after you've broken your back! There's a reason the doctor won't sign off on your returning to work! It's so you sit at home, not so you go out and do something ridiculous like buy a business that causes you to stand on your feet for hours a day and take on more stress!" Isa shrieked. She glowered at Ethan. "I told you it was a bad idea."

"I don't need to hear that. It was my decision."

"You do need to hear that. And, yes, it *was* your decision!"

"Yes, it was! You're the one who told me that over and over! You're the one who never wants to let our lives intersect in any real way."

"What in the world are you talking about?" Isa crossed her arms, her face hot.

"I wanted your input. I wanted to make this decision with you."

"Oh, please. You knew how I felt about it. Besides, we were barely dating! We're still barely dating!" Isa started pacing, then stopped, wishing she could stomp her foot, she felt so furious.

"We're not barely dating! It's been months! You know how I feel about you." Ethan struggled to stand back up.

"Stop. Just stop. I'm leaving." Isa stood still.

"You're not leaving. We're talking."

"We're shouting!" Isa yelled.

"Fine! We're shouting!" Ethan sat back down, cringing. Isa softened just a tad at the sight. She tried to steady her shaking voice.

"You shouldn't be working at the restaurant. I don't really understand why you're doing it."

"I can't stop," he said finally. "And you should understand that."

Isa blinked. "What do you mean by that?"

With bedhead hair and dark circles under his eyes, Ethan stared up at her and Isa felt the impulses to both run out the door and kiss him soundly.

Instead she stood frozen.

"I mean I'm used to being busy and when I'm not, suddenly I feel empty. I don't have a family like you do. I'm alone over here—don't you get that? I make decisions for myself without anyone else's involvement all the time. And I made this one. I bought this restaurant. Yeah, I knew you didn't want me to. But I wanted it. And while I want you, I never really know where I stand with you."

Isa trembled without warning at his words, *I want you*.

After that declaration, Ethan closed his eyes and laid his head back on the sofa.

"You want to be in a relationship with me now, Ethan.

How do you know you'll feel the same a few weeks from now? A few months from now?" Isa asked in a small, quiet voice.

He opened his eyes. "What do you want, Isa?" he asked without answering her questions.

You. She swallowed. "For my dad to be well, for my life not to feel so hectic, for God to answer my prayers. I want to feel happy at my job. To be married. To have children. To have one night's rest where I wake up feeling like I'm living the life I was meant to live. To wake up not feeling so tired. I'm tired of being tired. I want…I want an abundant life," her voice ebbed and flowed, her words starting with fervor and ending in only a soft mumble.

He leaned over, his elbows on his knees. Isa stared at his ruffled hair.

"What is that?" he asked.

"I don't even know anymore," Isa answered.

"Well…I know what I want, too. I want to be well again. I want to be strong again. I want to be a firefighter and run my own restaurant and have a girlfriend who understands me and wants me to be part of her life and who wants to be part of mine."

"I do want you to be part of my life," Isa said, taken aback.

"It doesn't always feel that way."

Isa tensed up. "Well, you say you want me. You say you want me to be part of your life. You say you want my input. But you've known all along I didn't want to date someone in the restaurant business. You've known I've thought you were taking on too much while you're still struggling to heal from your injuries. So my opinion doesn't seem to really matter all that much. And besides all that, you know I have so much going on in my own life right now—my work, my dad's health, my family, my friends—I don't even have time to sleep!"

"I know. We both have busy schedules, but it's different for you. Your life is full of family and people who love you. Mine is filled with my work. You have no idea what I'm going through. Maybe neither of us is ready for this kind of relationship."

Isa hadn't braced for that. She took the words like a punch to the stomach, full force.

I knew it. I knew it was too much to hope for. I knew I was in over my head. I knew it would never work out.

She took an unsteady breath. "Maybe you're right. I told you when we first met that you should concentrate on healing."

He looked up at her, his eyes red and rimmed with moisture. "Yes, you did. I haven't done a very good job of that, I know. But you don't know what it's like to be alone, Isa. To not have a family that cares for you."

Her mouth was dry and her heart hurt. "You have the guys, Ethan. Company 51 loves you."

"It's not the same," he said.

I love you.

The words stayed just below the surface.

God loves you. She could hardly remind him of that when half the time she doubted it herself.

God, where are you? The prayer came from her without warning. *God, I'm struggling here. This whole thing is falling apart just like I knew it would.*

Ethan leaned back on the sofa.

"Isa, I'm tired. I'm in pain. I can't do this right now."

Isa stepped back toward the door. "Me either. So let's not."

Ethan stared at her. "What are you saying? Let's not fight? Or…do you not want to be in a relationship with me?"

"Is that what this is?" Isa countered.

"I thought so," Ethan answered. He closed his eyes. "I'm too tired to fight with you, Isa."

"You don't have to," she said as she walked to the door and left.

Chapter 13

More than a week later, Isa followed Leo and Mandy into her parents' home. Her father had spent another night in the hospital after having had his second surgery for deep brain stimulation. The surgery had gone well and the family felt hopeful. Isa carried an overnight bag with her. Her mother had asked her to stay over a night or two just to make sure her father was all right. Desperately needing some rest, she'd taken two nights off to stay at her parents' home. She only hoped she'd get some sleep.

Once her father was resting comfortably, Isa sat silently on the swing outside while Leo prepared a quick lunch. She rocked back and forth out on the deck, taking in the far view of the mountains from where she sat.

"How long has it been?"

Isa looked up to see Mandy there, Tony drifting to sleep on her shoulder. She patted the seat next to her.

"Well?" Mandy pressed. Isa rocked next to her sister-in-law.

"Nine days."

"Ah," Mandy said.

Nine days since she'd walked out of Ethan's apartment. Nine days since she'd heard his voice, since she'd argued with him, since she'd seen him alone and in pain.

"Do you know yet?" Mandy asked. A cool breeze raced past them and danced across Isa's face. She closed her eyes and enjoyed the sun.

"Do I know what?"

"If you're in love with him."

Isa opened her eyes and looked at Mandy. "I don't know how I feel. Frustrated, I guess. I'm disappointed that we haven't talked."

"I would be, too."

"He's texted me, just asking about Dad and stuff like that. He's said we should talk soon, but he's not insisting."

"He's letting you cool off."

"I don't need nine days for that. I think it's more likely he's just really busy with the café. And he did say maybe neither of us is ready for this kind of relationship."

"What kind is that?" Mandy asked. Isa didn't respond but she knew the answer.

The kind that leads to more. The kind that leads to marriage and commitment and family. The kind that she was pretty sure they both wanted.

"So call him."

"No way," Isa stated, and Mandy barely smiled.

"Okay."

"You better be on my side about this," Isa warned.

Mandy nodded. "There's nowhere else for a Romano to be. I'm on your side. But I hate to see you lose something that might be incredible. You and Ethan—I watched you guys the day Maggie went into labor. It's like he's your match."

Isa shook her hair back and pressed her temples. A headache had crept up on her.

"I never wanted to date a guy who owned a restaurant."

Mandy laughed, then covered her mouth, trying to hold it in so she wouldn't wake Tony.

"What's so funny?"

Mandy smiled. "I was just thinking about the fact that I used to dream of dating a guy who owned a restaurant."

Isa grinned back at her. "Well, you got your chef in shining armor."

"I did," Mandy agreed. "Does Ethan want to give up being a firefighter? Does he want to run his restaurant full-time?"

"I don't think so. He loves being a firefighter. I think he's afraid he'll never be one again. But if he'd just stop and let his body heal, he could do it again. He's so stubborn."

"Hmm, I wonder what that's like," Mandy said playfully.

Isa gave her a Look. "Let's move away from the 'stubborn' topic. Don't you have any advice for me?" Isa asked.

"Sure. Pray."

Isa rolled her eyes. "I could be waiting a really long time for an answer."

Mandy didn't scoff. "Then how about I pray for you? The truth is I'm already praying, Isa. And Leo. And your mom and dad."

Isa bit her lip. She thought of her father saying he was hoping for good things for her.

"Are you living an abundant life, Mandy? Were you before you met Leo?"

Mandy rubbed Tony's back. "Yes. And maybe. I had a good life before I met Leo, Isa. But God knows what we need. And I needed Leo. My life was full before—but now it's so much better. There are ups and downs, but I wake up thanking God and I go to bed thanking God. I have hope and peace. Sometimes I feel guilty for feeling so happy. But I believe all good things come from the Father. So I just thank Him for the blessings in my life. And I remember the times God's been there for me. Those memories carry me through the not-so-easy days."

Isa was quiet.

"Think of a time when you knew without a doubt that God was there for you, Isa."

Isa bit her lip. "I can't think of one."

Mandy stood up. "Try. I'm going to lay Tony down in the guest room. Come in to eat soon, sis." She walked back to the house with Tony.

"Mandy," Isa said before she went inside. Mandy stopped and looked over her shoulder.

"What if he doesn't call? It *has* been nine days. What if he doesn't?"

"Then you have some decisions to make, Isa."

With Mandy gone, Isa tucked her legs under her on the swing. She watched the leaves rustle as wind blew through them and she let her mind wander, trying to think of a time when God had shown up for her in an unmistakable way. Before long her mother called out to her that lunch was ready and she went inside. But her mind kept wandering, and her soul stayed restless.

Ethan minced an onion and added it to the pot of beef stew that sat simmering on the stove. The café had been slow through breakfast, and he was already prepping for lunch. The scent of stew stirred a host of memories. It was one of the only recipes he had of his mother's. While she hadn't cooked all that much during his childhood, Ethan remembered her making beef stew every winter. It had been a favorite dish of his father's and she'd made it just the way he'd liked it. Ethan thought of her every time he made it, and even though he tried not to, he felt the loss of both her and his dad.

He added in garlic and a blend of spices and then raised the stove's heat just a tad.

The kitchen felt warm, filled with smells of different foods and the feeling of people coming in and out as waitresses flew in to grab plates. Ethan could hear the sound of Mark humming near him. But Ethan felt lonely.

I will never leave you.

Ethan stopped what he was doing.

Father, I miss Isabella. It was an honest admission. Ethan wasn't sure it qualified as a prayer. But it was true regardless. He missed her.

She'd stood in his apartment and yelled at him. He thought of her hands on her hips, the heightened tone of her voice, the fire in her eyes—in the moment, he hadn't realized what they'd signified. But alone, after she'd left, when his pulse had slowed and he'd thought over every word that had been slung between them, it had hit him.

She cared. She cared enough to fight with him.

He couldn't even remember the last time that he'd had someone in his life who cared that much—besides Company 51.

And she was right. He'd taken on too much. He couldn't heal if he couldn't rest.

The problem was…neither could she.

Ethan stepped outside through the back door for a quick breath of fresh air. He leaned against the building and talked to the only family member he had who cared about every detail of his life.

Father, I'm in pain. What do I do now? I've put off the MRI because every day I'm busy here at the café. But

*I can't keep doing that. I need help. It's just so impor-
tant to me that this café is a success. I'm responsible for
it. There's no one else. I've poured almost everything I
have into it.*

*And what do I do about Isabella? I can see how she'd
think that her opinion doesn't really matter to me based
on my decisions, but that's not true. I want to know her
opinion on everything. And it does matter to me.*

*Maybe it's just bad timing for the two of us. Maybe
when things slow down...*

"Hey, Chef. Orders are picking up," Mark said, stick-
ing his head out the door.

"I'll be right in," Ethan told him.

Lunch picked up and the café had a steady flow of
customers, but still Ethan was worried. Once the doors
were closed and he had time alone in his office to go
over the books, the numbers worried him. Mick had
told him that some months would be better than others.
He'd invested so much, he couldn't stop the anxiety that
hung over him like a cloud. What if the café didn't make
enough money? What if he couldn't go back to Company 51? What then?

There was a knock at the door and Jenny poked her
head in.

"The dining room is clean, Ethan. I'm leaving." She
walked in and set a bowl on his desk. "You never stopped
to eat. I set aside some stew for you before the kitchen
was cleaned."

"Thanks, Jenny!" Ethan took the bowl in his hands.

"No problem," she said before ducking out. Ethan sat
back, wishing he could somehow eradicate the pain in his
back, and breathed in the scent of the stew before taking a
generous bite. He savored the taste, thinking of his mother.

Along with the physical pain he felt, a sense of sorrow at the thought of his mother came over him.

I will never leave you.

The words from Scripture entered his mind again. A comforting and unwavering promise.

Chapter 14

Thursday afternoon Isabella waited impatiently for the elevator doors to open. Once they finally did, she rushed through and turned the corner, heading for the NICU. Pushing through the double doors, she jogged up the corridor to where she saw Maggie standing with the doctor. Maggie's face filled with relief at the sight of her.

"Hey," Isabella said as she came to a stop. "What's going on?"

"Bianca's running a fever. We were slated to be released today, but if her fever doesn't break, we probably won't be taking her home."

Isa nodded. "It's more important that she's healthy and ready, Mags. She'll be home before you know it."

Maggie took a deep breath and closed her eyes. After a moment, she opened them. "You're right, Isa. Of course. I just wish—"

Isa touched her friend's arm, her heart full of understanding for the mixed feelings she was probably experiencing. The doctor spoke to the two of them for a few more minutes and then left them alone with Bianca.

"Is José working?" Isa asked. Maggie nodded.

"He's working all the time. The medical bills, the regular bills—it's a lot, Isa. I keep thinking maybe I should go back to work to help out once my maternity leave is up. But then I see Bianca and I feel so strongly that my place is by her right now...."

"Mags," Isa said firmly. "Bianca's your daughter. *Of course* you feel like your place is by her. It's going to be okay. God will provide."

Isa bit her lip, praying for the faith to believe her own words. *You will, won't You, Father? You won't forsake them, right? You know their every need. I know You do. Please help them.*

Whether she wanted it to or not, her every thought seemed to turn into a prayer these days. By midnight that night Isa was rolling her shoulders and taking an aspirin for her stiff neck. The E.R. had been moderately busy, enough to keep her from feeling the exhaustion, but she couldn't quite shake the achiness coming over her. She leaned against the counter as she filled out paperwork. She sniffed, annoyed that her nose seemed to be running.

I'm just tired of being on my feet. A hot shower and a few hours of sleep and I'll feel better.

As Isa walked to her car after her shift, she made the immediate decision to head home instead of over to her parents' house. The ache had spread to her shoulders and she felt sure she needed sleep. Eight hours later she woke up, sat up in bed, then fell back onto her pillow.

"Tell me I'm not sick," she complained out loud.

What is this? Who gets a late-summer cold? The

weather hasn't even started to turn chilly! I have way too much going on in my life to catch a cold in August!

Isa took her temperature. A hundred and one. Achiness touched every part of her body and her head was pounding. Her nose ran like a waterspout. She wrapped her robe around her and checked the clock. It was a little after four o'clock.

Thank goodness it's Friday and I'm not on the rotation at work tonight. There's no way I could go in feeling like this.

She took some over-the-counter medicine she had in her cabinet and then climbed back into bed, pulling her comforter up to her nose as she shivered with chills. She called her mother just to be able to tell someone she felt sick, to hear her mother fuss over her and offer sympathy.

Then she fell back asleep and woke up around six, her throat now sore and her energy level lower than ever.

I miss Ethan.

Isa wanted to call him. She wanted him to come over with something delicious that he'd made, ready to take care of her. She tried to steer clear of the depressing notion that if she had a husband, she'd have a constant companion, someone to be with her through sickness and health. Someone to care for her. Again Isa thought about how different she'd expected her life to be by this point. She hated being alone.

Why hasn't he called? What's he waiting for? Isa couldn't understand it. She'd thought for sure Ethan would have called by now. He'd pursued her so intently— now one argument and he disappeared on her for two weeks? It was disappointing. She needed someone who could fight with her if necessary and who would always fight for her.

And she'd thought Ethan was that man.

A knock at the door caused her to jump. Isa carried a box of tissues with her to the front door.

"Mom!" she said with a surprised sniffle. Her mother walked in and set a paper bag on the counter.

"Isabella," she said, pulling Isa into a warm hug before holding her at arm's length to inspect her. "Have you taken medicine?"

"Yes, Mom," Isa answered. "You didn't have to come all the way over here."

Her mother immediately moved to begin washing the few dirty dishes in Isa's kitchen sink. "I wanted to. You need to eat. Look in the sack. I brought vegetable soup," she said over her shoulder. "There's a loaf of Italian bread to go with it."

Isa set out a plastic container of soup and the loaf of bread. Then she reached down and pulled out a leather-bound journal.

"Mom, what's this?" she asked.

"Oh, I was cleaning out the closet in the guest room, your old room, and I found that. It belongs to you."

"My journal from high school!" Isa said, clutching it. Her mom looked back at her and grinned.

"Don't worry. I didn't read it."

"Well, that's a relief," Isa said before setting it aside and taking a bowl from the cupboard for her soup. Her mother turned around, dried her hands on a dish towel and motioned for Isa to sit down. Too tired to protest, Isa did as her mother instructed. She sat on the sofa while her mother prepared a tray for her.

"Have you heard from Ethan?" her mother asked cautiously as she set the tray on the coffee table. Isa shook her head, reaching for the bowl and swallowing a spoonful of vegetable soup.

"This is delicious, Mom. Thank you."

"Are you going to call him?" her mother asked, folding her arms.

Isa nibbled on the chunk of bread from the tray and shrugged.

"Maybe. I mean, it's *possible* I might one day."

Her mother smiled, satisfied with the answer. "I wish I could stay longer, but your father needs me at home."

"How's Dad today?" Isa asked with interest. "Tell him I'm sorry I couldn't stop by."

"Isabella! You don't have to apologize. We know you have a life outside of us. We want you to. You don't have to come over so often."

"I don't mind. I want to," Isa insisted. "You're my family. If I'm not there for you, what good is family? Look at me. I'm sick and here you are, Mom. Helping me. That's how you raised me to be."

Her mother's face softened and she stepped closer, kissing the top of Isa's head. "Thank you for saying that. Well, your father is doing better."

"He really is, isn't he?" Isa echoed. Her mom perched on the arm of the easy chair.

"The surgery was successful. He's still showing a few of the symptoms, but still, the progress from how he was is remarkable. The best part has been how encouraged he seems. I've been afraid—afraid that maybe this is just a dream and any minute he'll be worse again." Her mother's voice was fraught with emotion.

"Mom," Isa said softly. "It's normal to feel that way. But he's doing better. We can all see it. He's talking easier, he's moving around easier, he's not shaking as badly."

"Yes, I'm grateful," her mother said even as her eyes were glossy with tears.

"I'm grateful, too," Isa said with a tug at her heart.

Later, after her mother had left and Isa had finished her soup, she made her way back to bed. Not quite drowsy enough for sleep but without much energy to do more than lie down, she took her old journal to bed with her and started to read. Most entries were typical high school drama—crushes, hurt feelings from girlfriends, annoyance with teachers and her parents, frustration with her appearance. But every now and then she'd find an entry that held more depth, that revealed more of Isa's teenage heart. About halfway through the journal, Isa heard a ping-pong noise come from her laptop on the nightstand, telling her she'd received a message.

She grabbed the laptop and settled back into her pillows. She opened the message through her social-networking page.

Hey. Do you miss me yet?

The smile on her face was instant. Ethan Carter.

Who are you again? she replied.

Firefighter/cook. Stubborn guy who buys restaurants on a whim when he's been badly injured.

Isa laughed out loud.

It's coming back to me now. How are you?

I'm okay. I keep thinking about this girl I know.

Isa sighed. A strong sense of relief coursed through her, along with the emotional flutters that Ethan always seemed to stir in her.

I was too hard on you. I'm sorry.

The apology came easy for her and Isa realized how badly she'd missed Ethan.

No, you were right. How are you?

Sick.

Sick over our fight?

She giggled as she typed.

You wish. I caught a silly summer cold. I'm home in bed with a fever and a box of tissues.

Can I come over?

She bit her lip.

Reread my line above. I AM SICK.

I'll risk it. I promise to bring chocolate.

No. I don't want you to get sick. So…why has it taken so long for you to call me?

She held her breath, waiting for his answer.

Will you be mad if I say it's because I've been working too much?

Yes.

Well, I ran into some issues at the restaurant.

If I had a dollar for every time I've heard that one...

Okay, okay. One of my waitresses got a better job offer and she subsequently quit. So we've been shorthanded and I've been scrambling to find a replacement. But I hired someone yesterday.

Isa didn't respond for a moment.

Isa? I also thought we needed some space.

Her heart hurt at that comment. Was he right? Had they needed space?

She didn't want space. Space made her nervous. In the past, "space" had always meant "time to reevaluate whether we're a good match" or "time to look for someone else."

Isa? You're making me nervous. Say something.

She took a deep breath. Maybe it was the cold medicine or just the fact that she felt crummy and weak. But she suddenly didn't feel able to keep being witty. To keep playing along. She needed something real. She started typing before she could talk herself out of it.

I was worried. I missed you, Ethan.

Isa counted the seconds while she waited for Ethan to respond.

I missed you first.

Chapter 15

Ethan looked through bleary eyes at the clock above his fireplace. Ten-oh-eight. He and Isa had messaged back and forth for just an hour before she'd needed to take more medicine and try to get some sleep. He'd fallen asleep on his sofa. He struggled to sit up, grumbling at the tightness in his back. Falling asleep on the sofa never did him any favors when it came to dealing with back pain. Feeling instantly guilty that he still hadn't gone in for an MRI, he forced himself to do a few of the stretches that Keira was always encouraging him to do and then ambled into the kitchen. After pouring a bowl of cereal, Ethan took it with him onto the tiny terrace of his apartment. He sat in the one chair that fit on the balcony and looked out at the night sky.

Chatting online with Isabella had told him several things. While he often appreciated space when feeling frustrated with people, Isabella did not. He thought back to her silence after his comment about needing space and he knew without words that space wasn't what she wanted.

He wondered if she needed it, though—time to think through her feelings and come to a conclusion.

And chatting with her had let him know something else: she'd missed him just as much as he'd missed her. Without saying a word directly about it, she'd somehow communicated to him that she wanted him to invade her space, not give her more of it. Ethan would file that away for the next time they had an argument. And with Isabella Romano, Ethan had no doubt there'd be a next time.

Why did I wait so long to contact her? he wondered. The truth was that he'd missed her from the moment she'd stormed out of his apartment. When it came to being flirty and persistent with Isa, Ethan didn't have a problem. Isabella always responded positively to his persistence. They were similar in that fashion. They both liked to tease and joke around. But when it came to feeling hurt and annoyed, Ethan tended to withdraw. He could see now that Isa needed the opposite kind of reaction from him. She wanted him to stick around when things were uncomfortable, not pull back.

Suddenly Mandy's words reverberated through his mind and made much more sense to him.

She'll need proof.

Ethan stared at the stars, quietly eating his cereal.

After he finished, he put the empty bowl in the sink and then went to bed, setting his alarm for 4:30 a.m. Breakfast came early at the café and he had a stop to make before work.

At six-thirty the next morning, Ethan stood at Isa's door, trying to text her while holding bags of food and flowers he'd managed to buy at the grocery store at six in the morning. He figured if she didn't respond, he'd just leave everything on her doorstep rather than wake her. But she texted back almost immediately.

I'm awake. What's up?

Come to your door. Do not fix your hair, he replied. Ten minutes later the door cracked open. Ethan sighed.

"I told you not to fix your hair, Isa."

"You don't know what I look like when I roll out of bed, Ethan Carter. I rival Medusa. So yes, I tied my hair in a knot. For goodness' sake, I'm still in pajamas."

They just stood there for a moment, Ethan with his arms full of stuff, Isa watching him. She hadn't been kidding when she'd said she was sick. Ethan took in her bloodshot eyes, red nose and pale skin.

"You're going to get sick. I'm still running a slight fever," she warned.

"Let me in," he said as he rolled his eyes.

She smiled at that and stepped back, pushing open the door.

"Lucky for you, my mom washed my dishes last night. So the place isn't a total wreck."

"Like I'd care, Isa," Ethan retorted, dropping the bags on the counter and handing her the flowers.

She accepted them graciously. "Are these I'm-sorry-I-took-so-long-to-call flowers or get-well flowers?" she asked as she found a vase in one of the cabinets.

"Both." The moment Isa turned around, Ethan kissed her, runny nose and all.

When he let her go, he wasn't sure if her eyes were watery from the illness or if she was almost crying.

"I should have called sooner," he whispered. She buried her head into his chest and nodded. "I'll know next time," he promised.

She pulled away and stepped to the other side of the counter, reaching for a tissue.

"You need breakfast," Ethan stated. "I made breakfast burritos this time. I also brought some white-bean chicken chili for lunch. It's a new recipe I've found and it's crazy how good this chili is. You'll love it. Just heat some up in the microwave. And I'll be back after the café closes. I'll bring dinner for us."

She shook her head. "You don't have to."

"I'm going to," he told her. "I'll decide on dinner. You get to pick the movie we watch. Just text me later and I'll pick it up."

"Saturday-night dinner and a movie?" He could see the glee in her eyes. "That sounds perfect," she said as she sniffed. He reached for her hand, pulled her close to him and kissed the tip of her red nose.

"Go, Ethan," she said with a sigh. "You've got a restaurant to run."

"I know," he agreed. "But I'll be back soon. We need to catch up. I want to hear all about how your dad's doing. And Leo and Mandy and everybody."

Isa was already biting into a burrito.

"Am I forgiven, Isa?" Ethan asked.

She wiped her mouth. "Am I?"

"There's nothing to forgive. You were just being honest with me."

"What made you finally message me?"

Ethan swallowed. "I'd missed you for a long time. I just needed to talk to you."

"You sort of disappeared on me, Ethan. That's happened to me before and it's not usually a good sign that the relationship is going to work," she said, her eyes fixed on him.

Ethan felt terrible. "Can I have a second chance?"

"To prove what exactly?"

Ethan smiled. "To prove that I'd rather fight with you than just plain talk with anybody else."

She tapped her lips.

"Well, Isa?" Ethan pressed.

"How can I say no to that?" she asked with a smile and then a sneeze. She reached for another tissue. Ethan just stared at her while she blew her nose and then had a coughing spell, the truth hitting him like a two-by-four. Without a doubt, he was completely in love with the pajama-clad woman sniffling in front of him. He wanted, maybe even needed, her to be a permanent fixture in his life.

Isa sneezed and carried a mug of tea with her to the sofa. She shook her head, frustrated that she couldn't shake the cold. She glanced at the clock. Too many hours until Ethan was coming back to bring dinner and watch a movie. She had nothing to do for the rest of the day. And with such a depleted energy level, there wasn't much she could do anyway.

She reached for the journal she'd dropped on the coffee table earlier and flipped to the entry she'd left off on. Many entries were just recaps of her days, but some entries were actually prayers she'd written out. Isa enjoyed reading those best.

Dear God,
Thanks for showing up for me today. I was beginning to worry.

Isa paused for a moment, her heart jumping at the words. She thought of Mandy's challenge that day at her parents' house to remember a time when God was there for her. She glanced at the month and year at the top of the page. The entry had been written during the first month of her eighth-grade year—the year her family had moved to Colorado. Not the easiest year of her life. Isa went back to the entry.

> As You know, I hate it here. I miss L.A. I miss my friends. I miss our house. I miss the staff at Romano's. I miss Patrick. I miss knowing where I belong.

Isa thought back to Patrick, her first ever "going steady" boyfriend. The relationship had consisted of sitting next to each other at lunch. With a chuckle, she remembered that it hadn't been quite strong enough to endure long distance. One phone call from Patrick and she'd never heard from him again. Isa kept reading.

> God, I still don't know why You let Dad bring us all out here. I hate starting over. I have to work in the restaurant every day after school. Why me? It was Dad's choice to move us to Colorado. Now I'm stuck here. I got a letter a couple of weeks ago from Grandma. I'd written her and told her how terrible everything is, and she wrote me back and told me she wants the two of us to pray every day that I'll make a really good friend. So I've prayed every day. And today…well…I think I made a friend. During third period—science, blah!—I sat next to Karen again. She's super quiet. She *never* talks. But today when Mr. Keegan told us to pair up for an assignment, I leaned over and asked her to be my partner. Seriously, she lit up like a Christmas tree. The girl obviously needs a friend as badly as I do. And we found that we work really well together! She asked me all sorts of questions about L.A. and my family.

And we made plans to study together at my house this Thursday.

I know just making a friend seems small. But I finally feel happy after feeling sad for weeks. And I think it's because You answered my prayer and helped me make a new friend today. Thank You.

Isa read the entry twice, a lump rising in her throat. It did seem small—but it also reassured her somehow. She kept reading. Looking back through teenage Isa's life humbled her. Even in middle and high school, her faith had been strong. Somewhere along the way, she'd grown cynical and tired. She'd stopped seeing God's work in her life. But entry after entry gave her glimpses into a girl who trusted God for even the small things. She read through and could picture living through those moments—asking to be forgiven for bad choices in high school, excited for God's work in her heart during church camp, needing help to know what to do when a friend started struggling with an eating disorder. Through the words on every page, Isa could see God working in her heart and life as a teenage girl. He was there for both the big and small moments.

After a while she rubbed her eyes and set aside the journal, feeling the weight of both past and present decisions.

God, did You stop showing up...or did I stop seeing You show up? I know one thing—I want to see You again. I need to sense Your presence the way I did when I was younger. I'm not that young girl with vibrant faith any longer. Things have changed.

In the silence of her apartment, with only the sound of her own sniffling and coughing, Isa wanted to be changed all over again. She wanted to be a woman who trusted God for even the small things.

It had taken a summer cold knocking her over for her to

have a few moments for real introspection. Nothing made her feel weak quite like fever, chills and a runny nose. And for some reason, weakness always pushed her back to God. Isa dug deeper under the throw blanket around her and held the journal to her chest.

I can't do it on my own, Father, she prayed. *But if You'll help me, I think I'm ready for a change. I can see how present You were in my younger years. To be honest, I haven't been able to see it so much in the past few years. What should I do?*

The answer in her heart was immediate.

Seek and you will find me.

Chapter 16

"That's it, guys! Thanks!" Ethan called out Monday morning as two men hopped back into their truck and pulled out from behind the café. He turned around and went back inside the kitchen, pleased to see his shelves stocked and replenished but, as usual, overwhelmed by the cost of all the food.

Mark was looking through the vegetables. "Everything looks really fresh. I'm excited to start cooking!" he said, tossing a tomato into the air. Ethan grinned.

"Excellent. I was thinking of adding a Cobb salad to the menu. What do you think?" Ethan asked. He put down his inventory clipboard and grabbed a crate of vegetables to take to the pantry.

"Sure. That sounds good," Mark replied, inspecting a head of lettuce.

Ethan lifted the crate and within seconds he couldn't hold it. An initial stabbing pain in his back radiated down his leg. He couldn't even shout; the pain was too intense. The crate, along with Ethan, went sprawling to the floor.

"Ethan!" Mark yelled, rushing over to where he lay on the floor.

Ethan gripped Mark's arm, trying to hold in the cry of pain he was feeling.

"My back—" Ethan gasped.

"Jenny!" Mark called out. Jenny rushed into the kitchen, her eyes suddenly wide at the sight of Ethan on the floor. "Run next door and grab one of the guys from the fire department. Now!" She disappeared back through the door.

"Can you move?" Mark asked.

With effort, Ethan shook his head. "I don't think I should—not until the guys get here," he managed to say. He was sure only a minute or two had passed since Jenny had rushed next door, but every second felt like an hour.

"Ethan!" The relief Ethan felt at the sound of Caleb's voice was palpable. "All right, buddy. Let's see what we've got here. Andrew, the backboard now." Ethan felt a neck brace being placed around his neck. Carefully, both firefighters then transferred Ethan to the backboard. Ethan closed his eyes and tried to concentrate on breathing rather than the pain in his back.

"What's the situation?" Ethan heard the chief's voice but didn't open his eyes.

"Ethan lifted a crate and then just sort of collapsed," Mark told them.

"Was he unconscious?" Andrew asked.

"No," Mark answered. "Just obviously in incredible pain. I'm not sure what happened."

Ethan moaned as they carried him on the backboard out of the kitchen.

"Ellie's bringing around the ambulance. We need to

get him to the hospital," the chief said, his words laced with the intentional calm Ethan had heard so many times.

"Mark," Ethan said, opening his eyes.

Mark stepped up. "Don't even think about the café. Everything's under control. I'll call in another cook."

"Ethan, tell me where you're hurting," Andrew, the EMT, instructed as they transferred the backboard onto the stretcher.

"Stabbing pain in my lower back. Something might have torn—I'm not sure," Ethan answered, still concentrating on breathing.

"No doubt connected to the fracture," Andrew stated.

"What's wrong?" Caleb asked.

"It could be a number of things—sheared disc, pinched nerve, tumor."

Ethan held his breath as the stretcher was loaded into the ambulance.

"Everything's going to be okay, Ethan," he heard Ellie, the other EMT, tell him. But with the severe hurt he was feeling, Ethan couldn't believe her.

"I'll meet you at the hospital, Ethan," Caleb told him. Andrew peppered him with questions on the way to the hospital—how long had he been in pain? Why hadn't he had an MRI yet? When was the last time he'd been seen by his doctor? When was his last physical-therapy appointment? Ethan answered him through gritted teeth, also suggesting pain medication might be a good idea right about now.

"I know the pain is bad, but we'll be at the hospital soon. They'll want to run tests—let's just wait till we get there. Do you think you can wait? Just a few more minutes, Ethan, and we'll be there," Andrew said. Ethan had closed his eyes in response and stopped answering questions.

He tried to redirect his attention from the fact that he

was terrified of the slightest movement. He thought of Isabella and the fun they'd had Saturday night. He'd shown up on her doorstep with a large pizza with everything on it, popcorn and the movie *Ever After,* Isa's choice. They'd eaten dinner side by side on the sofa, talking about Isa's father's progress and the café, and then they'd watched the movie together. Isa had taken her cold medicine before the movie began and had fallen asleep halfway through, her head on Ethan's shoulder. He'd sat frozen for the next hour, not wanting to wake her.

It was the kind of night he'd like to repeat…oh, maybe every night of his life.

The ambulance hit a bump in the road and Ethan let out a cry and balled his fists. Andrew touched his shoulder.

"Almost there, Ethan. We're turning in now."

Along with the pain that made it hard to even breathe, Ethan felt the familiar aggravation and disappointment with his situation. Why did this have to happen to him? He felt too young to have back pain for the rest of his life. He'd just about given up on being a firefighter—now he couldn't even lift a crate of vegetables. How was he supposed to work? The ambulance slowed to a stop and the doors opened, and Andrew began barking out a status update on Ethan as they pulled him from the back of the truck. Ethan's mind flashed back to the night he met Isabella. He could picture her in her scrubs the following day, leaning over him with that mischievous smile of hers.

C'mon, tough guy. You've got this.

Isa wrapped her hair in a towel and padded through the apartment in her bathrobe, thankful to finally be breathing through both nostrils. Progress! She changed into a pair of jeans and a T-shirt and sat down after taking one more round of cold medicine. She figured after three days stuck at home battling her cold, she should be able to go back on the schedule that evening. Her phone buzzed beside her but she didn't recognize the number.

"Hello?"

"Isabella? It's Caleb, Ethan's friend from Company 51. I wanted to let you know that Ethan's on his way to the Denver Health right now."

Isa froze, a chill running down her spine. "What happened?"

Father, please... Her heart began praying before Caleb even responded.

"He lifted a crate at the café and it was too much for him, I guess. I'm not sure what happened but he collapsed and our EMTs took him to the hospital. I'm on my way there now."

Irritation at Ethan for picking up something heavy, mixed with worry over the fact that he was hurting, surged in Isa. When would he ever learn? Even before hanging up, she'd picked up her purse and grabbed her keys. Locking the door behind her, she speed-dialed her mother's number and asked her to pray.

After being examined, Ethan was scheduled for an immediate MRI. After the MRI, he was admitted to the hospital and taken to a room. Caleb walked in.

"Have you heard from the doctor yet?" he asked.

Ethan shook his head. "No, but they finally gave me something for the pain. I know I'll hear from the doc once he sees the results of my MRI. Thanks for coming, by the way."

"No problem. I'm glad to be here. The chief had to get back to the station but I have firm instructions to keep him informed. Oh and Mark told me to tell you again not to worry about the café. He's got it."

"Yeah, but what about tomorrow? And the next day? What then?" Ethan said, the frustration spilling over. "Why can't I just get better and things go back to normal? Where is God in all this?" His voice rose.

Caleb stepped closer to the bed, seemingly unperturbed by Ethan's tone.

"He's right here in this hospital room with us, Ethan. He's *right here*," Caleb answered. "And it could be worse, you know. You haven't exactly followed the doctor's orders, buddy." Caleb raised his eyebrows. "Starting a new business when you're supposed to be healing isn't the best way to get back on your feet."

Ethan laid his head back on the pillow and accepted the truth that Caleb was speaking to him. "I know." After a moment, he added, "You sound like Isabella."

"She's right. And speaking of Isabella, she's in the waiting room."

Ethan looked up with interest. "Really? Will you tell her to come in?"

"Sure. What about the other half a dozen Italians waiting with her?"

Ethan blinked in surprise. Caleb grinned. "I think every Romano in the city is in the waiting room."

"You're exaggerating," Ethan responded.

Caleb shrugged. "Her family is with her."

That thought caused a boulder the size of a fire truck to rise up in Ethan's throat. That Isa was there for him didn't really surprise him. It pleased him, though he knew she'd be annoyed when she heard about him lifting a crate. But he knew Isa well enough to know she'd want to be with him if he were hurting. But that her family would show up at the hospital for him too... He felt tears fill his eyes.

"Hey," Caleb said, keeping his eyes on the doorway,

pretending not to notice Ethan's tears. "I'm going to go get your girlfriend."

"Caleb—wait," Ethan said, getting hold of his emotions. Caleb turned. "What's an abundant life?" he asked.

Caleb looked surprised. "It's a life lived to glorify God. It's when you follow God's leading and you reap the rewards."

Ethan sighed. "I guess I'm not living one, then."

Caleb smiled and leaned against the edge of the bed. "Easy doesn't run parallel with abundant, Ethan. But it does mean you're never alone. Try to hold on to the promise that God can make all things work together for good for those that love Him. You're going through a difficult time right now, but that doesn't mean you're not right where God wants you. And it doesn't mean good things aren't still in store for you."

At that moment, Isabella walked through the door, her nose still a little red from all the sneezing she'd done in the past seventy-two hours. And despite her narrowed eyes— she was obviously unhappy to see him back in the hospital—Ethan couldn't help thinking that a key factor for him living an abundant life might have just entered his hospital room.

"If you weren't lying in a hospital bed, Ethan Carter, I'd yell at you right now," she said, her arms crossed.

Ethan withheld the smile he felt. Instead he nodded contritely as Caleb ducked out of the room.

"I know. But I *am* in the hospital, Isa," he said, hoping his pitiful state would soften her clear infuriation. He couldn't blame her. He was just as frustrated with himself at that moment.

"So I won't yell at you till you're feeling better. Caleb said you were lifting a crate or something?" Isa asked, immediately checking his monitors.

"Yeah. Stupid, I know. I didn't even think. I was feeling fine, so I grabbed the crate. Next thing I know, I'm on the ground, my back killing me."

She nodded.

"So Caleb said your family's here?" Ethan said, clearing his throat.

"Mom and Dad and Mandy are here. Mandy has Tony with her, of course. Caleb called me while you were on the way to the hospital. So I basically called everyone I know."

"Your Dad's here?" Ethan repeated, shocked.

Isa reached down and took Ethan's hand in hers.

"He insisted on coming. And he's doing so much better, Ethan. He wanted to be here for you."

Ethan felt the already-unsteady wall surrounding his emotions break inside of him. He sucked in a shaky breath and tried not to cry. Isa sat on the bed next to him.

"I'm not used to…family showing up for me," he stammered.

She nodded with understanding, still holding his hand.

"Why do you have to be so stubborn?" she whispered.

He sighed. "I don't know. I've taken on too much. And now what am I going to do about the café, Isa? I have to be able to run it. I've invested so much. I could lose everything." Ethan's voice cracked.

"Hey," she said softly. "Listen to me. Everything will be fine. I know you're overwhelmed right now. But you haven't even heard what the doctor has to say yet. Don't borrow trouble. Let's wait and see what can be done. As for the café…God knows your situation, Ethan. He'll provide a way."

Ethan cocked his head to the side, a half smile creeping onto his face. "Do you believe that, Isa?"

She looked down at their entwined hands. "I'm starting to."

"Thank you for coming." He squeezed her hand.

"Do you know why I'm really here, Ethan?" she asked. He didn't answer. "Because *this*—" she motioned to the two of them "—this is real for me." Her voice was quiet and Ethan could see her struggle with the vulnerability of her words. "I'm never going to want whatever this is going on between us to end. I don't think I'm ever going to get tired of fighting with you and making up with you and talking and laughing with you."

The pain, the stress, the fear—all of it seemed irrelevant compared to the pounding of Ethan's heart as he listened to Isa's words.

"Isa, I want you to know that I—"

The door slid open and Ethan's doctor walked in.

"Hi, Ethan, Isabella," Dr. Nichols said as he walked in. He stood at the end of the bed. "So it looks like we have things to talk about, Ethan. I assume you want me to continue with Isa here?"

Ethan nodded, tightening his grip on Isa's hand. "Yes, please."

"You have insufficient bony union of the L4 vertebra and it has caused a nerve entrapment of the nerve root." At the blank look on Ethan's face, Dr. Nichols slowed down and tried to explain. "Ethan, when you lifted the crate, your vertebrae compressed, or 'pinched,' the nerve. That's where the sharp pain came from. The MRI showed us that there's inflammation on the nerve. Also, we now know that your vertebra hasn't properly healed. This was missed on the X-ray, unfortunately. The good news is that we can fix this. The bad news is that this means surgery and more physical therapy."

"What does the surgery consist of?" Ethan asked.

"We'll need to have a neurosurgeon perform a lumbar foraminotomy, which will widen the space where the nerve root exits the spinal column and possibly fuse the vertebrae back together. You will continue physical therapy after surgery. You're looking at eight or more weeks of recovery, Ethan. And this time, when I say take it easy, I need you to take me literally on that. *If* you cooperate and let your body rest and focus on therapy, I still expect you to make a full recovery."

"When will you do the surgery?"

"As soon as we can. I'm hoping we can schedule you for first thing in the morning. After a day or two in the hospital, if there are no complications with the surgery, you can go home."

Ethan let the words sink in: *Eight or more weeks of recovery.*

The café.

As much as he liked Mark, Ethan wasn't sure he felt comfortable handing over his entire livelihood to him after just a couple of weeks of working together. But what choice did he have? Eight weeks? He couldn't close for that long. More medical bills. More café bills. The stress of his predicament inundated his entire body. Ethan inhaled and felt tense all over.

Dr. Nichols told them he'd schedule the surgery and disappeared down the hallway. Isa squeezed Ethan's hand.

"Are you okay? What are you thinking?" she asked.

Father, You helped me before. I could really use Your help right now.

Ethan held her hand tight. "I'm worried about the café," he acknowledged.

She touched his face and kissed his forehead.

"I'm more worried about *you.* The café isn't going anywhere. It's going to be okay, Ethan."

"Will you pray, Isa?" he asked weakly.

Isa smiled. "Are you sure? You know me—my prayers tend to become unreasonable outbursts."

That brought a smile to his face. "I'll chance it."

Chapter 17

Isa stayed at the hospital all night, sleeping on the cot in Ethan's room. She'd called in a friend to cover her shift. By six o'clock the next morning, she sat up and stretched, desperately needing coffee. Ethan's surgery was scheduled for 8:00 a.m. She looked over at him asleep in the hospital bed and got to her feet, arching her back and yawning. They'd talked well into the night—about the café, about the surgery, about their relationship. Isa needed time to process all that had been said between them. She headed to the cafeteria in search of a hot cup of anything caffeinated. Time to process proved impossible, seeing as how everywhere she turned, she knew people. She had to explain about Ethan's surgery over and over to her colleagues. She headed back to Ethan's room as quickly as possible and was glad to see him awake.

"Nervous?" she asked, sitting down on the edge of the bed. He shook his head.

"At this point, I just want to feel stronger, Isa. Whatever it takes."

"Does that include following the doctor's orders and letting your body heal?" she said, her eyebrows raised.

He nodded. "Absolutely. I've learned my lesson. I'm just not sure what to do about the café."

Isa frowned. "Ethan, one thing at a time. Let's get you through surgery, then tackle the problem of what to do about the café."

"Do I at least get a kiss before I'm wheeled off to go under the knife?"

Isa laughed. She leaned over and kissed him. "I'll be here when you wake up," she promised. Ethan nodded silently. The laughter and ease in the room faded with the looming surgery. Isa brushed Ethan's hair from his forehead, remembering the first night they met. "You're not alone. You know that, right? I'm here. And God's here."

Surprisingly, the reminder comforted her as much as she could see it surely comforted Ethan. The crinkle in his brow smoothed and he took a deep breath.

"You're right. God's got this."

Once he was taken out for surgery, Isa walked slowly back toward the waiting room, her heart overwhelmed. She wasn't afraid necessarily, though she knew all surgery included risk. Her thoughts shifted to Ethan's forthcoming recovery. He'd be unable to work for weeks. She understood the pressure of restaurant life. And she understood the huge financial investment that came with such a venture. No wonder Ethan was worried about what would happen to the café.

God, please provide help for Ethan. Please don't let him lose all he's invested.

Isa turned the corner to the waiting room and stopped in her tracks. Her mom and dad sat together, talking quietly with Maggie and José. Leo looked half asleep on one of the sofas, and next to him Mandy sat with her eyes glued to her phone. Baby Tony slept in a car seat on the floor. Isa's cousin Angelina was flipping through the channels on the waiting room TV.

Her mom looked up. "Isabella! How's Ethan?"

The sight of her family already in the waiting room so early in the morning flooded Isabella's heart. Tears came without notice and rolled down her cheeks. Within seconds her mother and Mandy and Maggie and Angelina were surrounding Isa, cooing and fussing over her as though she were a child. Leo stood with a worried look on his face.

"Is something wrong? What's happened to Ethan?"

Isa shook her head and wiped the stream of tears from her face. "No, he's okay. I mean, they took him into surgery but he should be fine. It's just—I didn't expect you all to be here."

"Isabella, we're Romanos. Where else would we be at such a time?" Leo said. Baby Tony squirmed and made a peep and Mandy moved to check on him. Isa sat down sandwiched between her mom and dad and laid her head on her dad's shoulder.

"Dad," she whispered, "I love Ethan."

He smiled and took her hand in his. "I know. And I love you."

A wave of more tears came over Isa.

I see it now, Father. Your presence. In the fact that my dad can even be here. In the love of my family showing up for me without me even calling. In the incredible man You've brought into my life who needs my help.

Isa blinked.

She knew what she had to do.

"I need to run down to the E.R. for a little while," Isa stated, standing up. She looked over at Maggie. "Mags, come find me if there's any update on Ethan." Her friend nodded.

"Text me if you need me," Maggie said. Isa took off toward the elevator.

Ethan opened his eyes.

"Hi there, Ethan. How do you feel?"

Ethan recognized the woman speaking to him as one of the nurses he'd met earlier. Karen was her name, or maybe it was Melissa. He couldn't remember.

"Groggy," he answered.

She nodded. "That's normal. The surgery is over and you're in your recovery room now. Dr. Chong is on his way to talk with you. I'm going to go let your friends and family know that you're awake. I'm under strict instructions from Isa." She winked at him and left the room.

Friends, not family.

Ethan tried to shake off the uninvited depressing thought. He was lucky to have such good friends. He was lucky to have Isa.

But...Father, just once it would be so nice to have family of my own.

"Ethan."

He opened his eyes again. Isa leaned over him, inspecting every inch of him, her eyes darting back and forth to the monitors.

"How are you?" she asked.

"I've had better days, I guess," he said, and she sat back with a chuckle.

"I bet."

The door slid open and Dr. Chong, the neurosurgeon who had performed Ethan's surgery, walked in, a smile on his face.

"Ethan! Welcome back." He stepped close to the bed.

His eyes scanned the chart in his hands before he looked up at Ethan and Isabella. "We've got good news. The surgery went well. Everything looks good. We're going to keep you here overnight for observation, but I think you can go home tomorrow. I'm recommending you wear your back brace for a few days just as a precaution. But I'm pleased with the results of the surgery."

Relief washed over Ethan. Once Dr. Chong had again stressed his instructions for recovery to Ethan, most of which involved therapy and rest, he left. Ethan looked around the room, noticing for the first time the balloons and flowers.

"Company 51 sent the balloons," Isa explained. "The Romanos sent the wildflowers. Oh, and a bouquet came from Redeemer Community Church, as well. The associate pastor stopped by while you were still in surgery. Mark and Carson and the girls at the café sent flowers, too."

"That was nice of them," Ethan said, still trying to pull himself out of the emotional rut he'd fallen into. "I think… I need some rest, Isa," he said, hoping she wouldn't feel offended.

"Of course you do," she said soothingly. "But could you see a few visitors first? The chief is here."

"Okay," Ethan agreed. "Tell him to come in."

Isa kissed the top of Ethan's head and rushed back toward the waiting room. Ethan laid his head back onto the pillow and closed his eyes, wishing he didn't feel so low.

"Ethan!"

His eyes fluttered open at the sound of people pouring into the room. His jaw dropped as most of Company 51 squeezed into the room, along with Isa's family.

"I don't think they allow this many visitors!" he said.

Isa glanced behind her toward the hallway. "He's right, everybody! You won't be able to stay long."

Isa's mother came over to him. She kissed his cheek and told him how glad they were that the surgery went well. Gabriel Romano sat in a wheelchair by the bed. He gave Ethan a warm smile and patted his arm.

Within moments a nurse came in to shoo out the rowdy crew of Company 51. Ethan didn't mind the noise. He appreciated the roomful of people.

"Thanks for coming," Ethan said to the chief as the guys filed out of the room.

"You're family, Ethan. Family sticks together. I look forward to seeing you back at the house when you're ready," Chief Rawlins told him.

"Thanks, chief," Ethan said, clearing his throat to keep the tears at bay.

"We'll be back soon, Ethan," Mandy said, bouncing Tony in her arms. "Leo's going to send over dinner from Romano's for you tonight."

Ethan smiled. "Sounds great. Thanks, you guys."

"Anything you need, Ethan, we're here," Leo said sincerely.

Ethan just nodded, unable to speak. Next to him, Isa found Ethan's hand and locked their fingers together. Everyone said their goodbyes and left the two of them alone.

"So that's what family feels like," Ethan said, his words breaking.

Isa rested her head on his shoulder.

"You should get used to it, Ethan. None of us are going anywhere."

Chapter 18

Isa fluttered around Ethan's apartment, arranging the many bouquets of flowers and organizing the freezer filled with meals from Leo and Mandy.

"Isa," Ethan called from where he sat on the sofa. "You're going to be late if you don't leave now."

"I know," Isa said. She stopped what she was doing and walked over to him. "I'm leaving."

"Tell Maggie and José I wish I could be there."

"They know," Isa assured him. Bianca was being released from the hospital and Isa wanted to be there to see it. "I'll be back later before my shift tonight. So don't do anything. Just watch TV and text me if you need me to come back earlier."

"I'll be fine," Ethan insisted.

Isa left in a hurry. Minutes later she pulled into the hospital parking lot and ran to the entrance just in time to see Maggie and José walking slowly toward the front door.

"Isa! You made it!" Maggie's smile widened. José ran ahead to pull the car around and the two girls sat at a bench together by the door. Bianca still looked tiny in the car seat Maggie was carrying.

"I bundled her up. She's so little," Maggie said.

Bundled was a bit of an understatement, in Isa's opinion. Bianca couldn't have caught a chill if there'd been one in a thirty-mile radius. But Isa just smiled.

"How's Ethan doing?" Maggie asked.

"He's okay. He just got home yesterday and he's already feeling bored today. But don't worry. I'm not going to let him do anything crazy like buy a new business."

Maggie chuckled. "So what's happening with you guys? Things seem to be getting serious."

Isa shrugged. "We'll see, I guess. He needs me right now."

Maggie touched Isa's shoulder. "And what about you, Isa? Do you need him?"

"I really care about him, Mags," Isa said. "I keep hoping... How do you know if a relationship will last?"

"Relationships last because people *make* them last, Isa," Maggie said, her words soft and kind but honest. "It doesn't just happen. It takes work. It takes sacrifice, forgiveness, loyalty and grace."

José pulled the car up and Maggie asked Isa to take some pictures as they loaded Bianca into the car for the first time. Happy to oblige, Isa took several photos and then hugged Maggie tightly before she and José climbed in their SUV. Isa waved as they drove away. She thought of the excitement of entering the hospital as a couple and then leaving as a family of three. She wondered if such a day would ever be in her future.

Isa stopped by the café on her way back to Ethan's apartment. There were more customers than she would have expected for so late in the afternoon. She immediately started helping bus tables. She passed Jenny on the way back to the kitchen.

"Thanks, Isa. We've been busy today," Jenny told her as they rubbed shoulders coming in and out of the kitchen.

"I can tell!" Isa said.

She waited till after closing to talk to Mark. "We've got to have more help if Ethan's not coming back anytime soon. Carson is only part-time," he said.

"I know. Ethan knows, too. I'm going over there as soon as I leave and I'll talk to him."

Mark nodded. Isa finished helping the girls clean the dining room and then left for Ethan's. Checking the clock, she knew she'd need to rest sometime before her shift.

She heated up one of Leo's frozen meals and then sat on the love seat across from where Ethan sat on the sofa while they ate dinner together.

"The café was busy when I stopped by." Isa broached the topic carefully.

Ethan's eyes brightened. Then his brow furrowed.

"Was Mark able to handle the rush?"

"He needs help," Isa said.

Ethan nodded. "I'll have to hire someone."

"I have someone in mind," Isa said, her eyes on the fettuccini on her plate.

"Really?" Ethan asked, interested. "Who? Do they have experience cooking or waiting tables?"

"Oh, both. Lots of experience."

"Sounds good. Can you get me a résumé?"

"Sure. But I'll have to update it. My current job history is more medical than culinary."

Ethan looked confused. "You're talking about…you? You have a job, Isa."

She set her plate on the coffee table and looked at Ethan.

"Just hear me out. You need help. I'm willing. You don't have to say yes, of course. It's up to you. But I've talked to my supervisor and I can cut down my hours. I'd only be working one night shift every other week. The rest of the time, I can work at the café. I can cook, if that's where you need me most."

"Could you also be the manager?" Ethan asked. Isa paused in disbelief.

"You want me to oversee the café and the workers?"

He nodded. "I trust you more than anyone, Isa. I know you'll do a great job."

Isa let those words sink in.

"So…you're saying yes?" she asked.

"I'm saying thank you. And I insist on paying you, but I'm not sure I can match what you're making at the hospital."

She smiled. "Lucky for you, I'm willing to work for less."

"Charity case, am I?"

She laughed. "Does that bother you?"

"Not if it means you're going to be working at my café." Isa kept giggling.

"What's so funny?" Ethan wondered.

"I'm just thinking of how Leo and my father are going to react to the news that I'm now cooking for and managing a café. I've balked at the thought of working for Romano's ever since I graduated high school."

"I know you're not a fan of restaurant life, Isa. The fact that you're willing to do this for me—well, it means a lot," Ethan said seriously.

The laughter faded from Isa, but the smile remained. She liked Ethan's ruffled hair, the intense look in his eyes, the Company 51 T-shirt that was obviously his favorite, gauging by the fraying sleeves and holes near the neckline. In short, she liked everything about Ethan. She liked him so much that working in his kitchen didn't even sound like a sacrifice to her.

"I'll talk with Mark tomorrow and ask him to show you how to make all the menu items. I know you'll catch on quickly. I mean, you practically rewrote the recipe for my corn chowder."

"True," Isa said with a dramatic sigh.

Isa spent the next few days shadowing Mark and cooking more than she had for the past several years. She'd forgotten how much work it was to produce enough food to feed a restaurant filled with people. After training with Mark, she'd go back to Ethan's apartment and continue practicing for hours, with Ethan to direct her and make sure she was making each dish according to what he wanted.

Her first morning as manager/chef of the Second Chance Café found Isa to be a nervous wreck. She arrived early, trying to steady her nerves as she prepped her workstation. She walked around the empty kitchen, drinking an espresso while memorizing every corner of the kitchen.

Father, I can't believe I'm doing this. I didn't expect to be so scared. What if I can't run this kitchen?

Isa nearly jumped out of her skin at the sound of a knock on the exit door. She glanced at the clock and realized that the knock probably came from Mark. She walked over and opened the door.

"Leo!" she cried, throwing her arms around him. "What are you doing here?"

"Is that an espresso?" he asked. "I'd love one."

"Come with me to the coffee bar. Now, I repeat, what are you doing here? It's the crack of dawn!"

Leo sat perched on a barstool while Isa made him an espresso.

"I'm here because *you're* here. I'm not going to miss my sister's first day as a chef."

The catch in Isa's throat was immediate. She swallowed hard. "I'm terrified," she confessed.

Leo seemed unfazed. "Of course you are. This is a big deal. You don't want to mess things up."

Isa crossed her arms. "Thanks for the vote of confidence. I feel *so* much better now."

Leo sipped his espresso. "You're not going to mess up, Isa."

"How do you know?" Isa asked meekly.

"Because being in the kitchen is second nature to you. And I know from experience how bossy you can be. In other words, you're a natural-born leader, little sister. Don't let your nerves tell you otherwise. Don't forget, I've tried to get you to work for me for years. I know you've got the Romano-family instinct when it comes to cooking."

Isa smiled, absorbing her brother's confidence in her. "I couldn't handle you trying to tell me what to do and you know it."

Leo laughed. "That's for sure."

"Do you have any tips for me?"

"Yes. Make sure you enjoy your work. And don't forget to eat. There were so many times that I worked hours upon hours without stopping to eat. The result is a chef who barks orders at people and has a short temper. Take breaks. Hydrate. Ask for help. Delegate. You're the one who reminded me to delegate, Isa. And it was good advice."

"I just can't believe I'm doing this. I've avoided restaurant life for as long as I've had a choice in the matter. But here I am, back in the kitchen."

Leo chuckled. "And Ethan didn't even have to ask. You just volunteered for him."

"I guess you're right." A tiny smile made its way to Isa's face. "Leo, thanks for showing up for me this morning." Isa looked across the bar at her older brother and a million pictures raced across her memory. She could see them at the breakfast table when they were still in elementary school; she could see Leo teaching her to play basketball; she could picture them racing down the stairs together every Christmas morning during her childhood.

Her heart twinged at all the memories. She loved her brother. And the fact that he was sitting at the Second Chance Café coffee bar at five in the morning told her how much he loved her.

Seek and you will find me.

Isa closed her eyes for a moment. *Thank You, Father. You sent my big brother to be with me, to help calm my nerves, didn't you? I know You're here with me, too.*

"I need to finish prepping," Isa told Leo, glancing at her watch. Leo downed the rest of his espresso, then slapped the top of the bar and stood up.

"Let's prep, then, Isa."

"If you're staying, I'm putting you to work," Isa warned him.

"Just tell me where you want me, Chef," Leo answered.

Chef.

Isa tied her apron around her waist and waved as Mark entered the kitchen. She took a deep breath. All the butterflies in her stomach couldn't squelch the feeling that she was exactly where she wanted to be. The Second Chance Café needed her. And maybe more importantly, Ethan Carter needed her.

Chapter 19

Isabella pulled into the Redeemer Community Church parking lot and stepped out of her car. She looked back as Ethan climbed out of the passenger side.

"Are you okay?" she asked, and Ethan scowled.

"I'm not an invalid, Isabella Romano."

"I know, but you need to let me know if you start hurting. I can take you back home. It's only been about two weeks since your surgery, Ethan."

"I'm okay for now. I promise to tell you if I'm in pain." Ethan reached for her hand and they walked into the church together. This time Isa waved back at the people she recognized and didn't hesitate when it came to smiling and greeting the people around her. She sat next to Ethan.

"So do you feel at home yet?" Ethan asked as the music began to play.

Home? Home with you?

"What do you mean?" Isa asked.

He nudged her shoulder. "You once told me you liked my church. I'm wondering if you're ready to make it your church, too."

Oh, that.

She nodded with a shy smile. "You don't mind, right?"

"It's *church,* Isa. The more, the merrier, you know? That's the general rule." Ethan tightened his grip around her hand. "But I'll be pretty disappointed if you don't promise to sit next to me every Sunday."

"We'll see," Isa said with intentional nonchalance, and Ethan smiled. The worship music swelled, and they stood with the crowd. That thirsty feeling came back over her. The desire to be filled up. The music, the message the pastor shared, the community around her—Ethan was right. She *was* beginning to feel at home at Redeemer Community Church.

Father, maybe I don't want to lose this thirsty feeling. Maybe I want to keep feeling it. I think it means I'm desperate for more of You. I've pushed You away for so long…. Now I want You back. Isa blinked at the realization. The music surrounded her and her hands lifted up in worship. Her eyes closed and she felt a sense of being found.

I wondered why I felt like I was waiting for someone else, Father, even after I met Ethan. But it's not about Ethan, is it? It's about You and me. I was waiting to feel Your presence again. And all along, You were waiting for me to come back to You.

In that moment, despite the fact that the congregation was singing a song that Isa had sung many times before, she felt as though a new song was born inside her.

"Isa?"

Isa looked over at Ethan. He'd leaned down close and spoken into her ear. She hadn't realized she was crying.

"Everything okay?" he asked.

She wiped her tears and nodded. "Everything's *really,* really good, Ethan."

He wrapped an arm around her and pulled her closer to him as worship ended and they sat down together.

After church services, the two of them went to Mandy and Leo's home for lunch. Isa held Tony in her arms while Mandy and Leo cleared the table. Tony had fallen asleep, so Isa carried him upstairs. Once he was in his crib, she walked through the kitchen, stopping to refill her glass of lemonade. She could hear Leo talking with Ethan in the dining room. Isa paused for a moment.

"So how is recovery coming along, Ethan? I know it can be discouraging—starting over with therapy."

"I *was* discouraged at first. But the truth is that Isa's positive spirit really bolsters me. She's always reminding me that God's with me. She's always telling me that I'll get through this, that I'll get stronger. She helps me keep a good perspective."

Isa couldn't move.

"Isa's an encourager. With all that's happened with my dad, my family relies on her so much. She keeps calm. She manages to stay positive. She's made a huge difference for my parents and for me as we've gone through this experience with my dad's health."

"She's certainly made all the difference in my life over the last few months."

"Isa!" Isa heard Mandy call her name. Isa walked to the dining room. "Could you bring out the blueberry cobbler?" Mandy asked.

"Of course," Isa answered, disappearing back into the kitchen. Ethan's words kept replaying through her head as she grabbed dessert. She took the pan of cobbler to the dining room, stopping for a moment to take in the sight of

Ethan sitting with Mandy and Leo, laughing and talking. He gave her an easy smile.

Everything about their relationship felt like love. Looking at that easy smile of his, hearing him talk about her in such a way that made her feel treasured, seeing him so comfortable with her family, knowing that her return to church had a lot to do with Ethan's simple invitation—Isa knew she loved Ethan. And she knew instinctively that this kind of love was meant to last. She just needed to hear Ethan say the words.

Monday morning Ethan went to therapy and then decided to stop by the café for lunch. Isa had insisted he wait a few days before coming in. She'd nicely told him she needed a couple of days on her own with the staff. He knew she really wanted to get a handle on running the place without the added pressure of having him over her shoulder every minute.

He was pleased to see that at noon most of the tables were occupied by customers. Caleb stood at the counter, picking up an order to go.

"Hey! Long time no see. How're you doing, man?" Caleb asked.

Ethan nodded. "All right. Therapy isn't easy, but I'm determined to follow the doctor's orders and heal properly this time."

"I'm sure you will," Caleb said. "We still miss you at the fire station, bro. And Isabella's doing a great job over here. I've been over several times and the food tastes just as good as ever. In fact, I think her meat loaf might be better than yours."

Ethan grinned. "I wouldn't doubt it. I think I'll sit down and order a plate."

"I've gotta get back to the house," Caleb said, nodding

toward the fire station. "Why don't you come by after you leave here? Everybody would love to see you."

"I might do that. See you, Caleb."

Ethan took a seat and waited for a waitress, browsing the menu he knew by heart.

"What can I get you?"

He looked up, shocked to see someone he hadn't hired. He cocked his head to the side and tried to remember where he'd seen her before. She looked so much like Isabella that he knew they had to be related.

"I'm Angelina," she said with a smile. "Isabella's cousin."

"Oh, right! Um, hi. Are you...working here now?"

She laughed. "No. I'm a manager at Romano's. One of the waitresses here called in sick this morning and Isa couldn't find anyone to replace her. She called Leo and he sent me over to help out."

"Wow, well, thanks for that."

"Having relatives in the restaurant business can come in handy, you know?" she said with a wink.

Ethan smiled good-naturedly. "Absolutely. I'll keep that in mind. I'd like to order the meat-loaf sandwich. But don't tell Isa it's for me, okay?"

Angelina shook her head. "Sorry, pal. I'm a Romano. I know where my loyalties lie."

They both laughed as she walked toward the kitchen.

After finishing his meal, he had to admit that Caleb was right. Isa's meat-loaf sandwich tasted delicious. He could tell intuitively that she'd tweaked the recipe. The thought made him smile.

She's putting her mark on this place.

Ethan waited until the dining room was nearly empty before going into the kitchen. He leaned against the counter while Isa wiped down the surface.

"So how does it feel to be working at a restaurant again, Isa? Be honest."

She tossed the dish towel in a basket to be washed and pulled out a barstool to sit on, then reached for a plate of food on the large kitchen island. "I told Mark to save me a plate from lunch," she said as she pulled off the plastic wrap. "I'm going to go ahead and tell you that you were right—I'm a huge fan of this white-bean chicken chili. Actually, with the weather turning a bit colder these days, everyone seems to be a fan of this chili."

Ethan pulled up a stool next to her. "Are you avoiding my question?"

She shook her head as she took a generous bite. He waited patiently.

"It's actually been better than I thought," she answered after a moment. "I forgot how much fun it can be working with a kitchen like this at my fingertips. And I haven't experienced the adrenaline boost of a lunchtime rush in a long time. And there's something else that I like about working here."

"What's that?" Ethan pressed.

"I'm the boss."

Ethan sat back and let out a belly laugh. "How did I not anticipate that?"

She shrugged. "I'm used to working with my dad or Leo. And while I wouldn't say they *ever* were able to boss me around, I had to work a lot harder for my voice to be heard."

"Well, Caleb tells me your meat-loaf sandwich is better than mine."

Isa looked sheepish. "I made a few tweaks."

Ethan pretended to be annoyed. "Are we going to fight over every recipe now?"

"Only if you insist," Isa quipped back at him.

Ethan kissed her before she could say another word.

"No fair! No kissing while arguing," Isa said after a moment.

Ethan didn't budge. He just leaned close to her.

"Isa, thank you for running my café while I can't," he said in a soft voice.

Isa touched Ethan's face. "I'm glad to do it. And really, I'm enjoying the work. I think I'm rediscovering my love for cooking. In fact, I know I am."

"Speaking of discovery, I've discovered that I love you, Isabella Romano."

Ethan wished he could somehow capture the stunned look on Isa's face.

Isa's lips curved into a full smile. She kissed Ethan's cheek.

"I loved you first."

Chapter 20

"Things are looking good, Ethan," Keira said as she hooked up his heat and stem treatment.

Ethan wiped beads of sweat from his forehead. "I can feel myself getting stronger. But to be honest, I'm still worried. The strength I need to perform my duties as a firefighter—well, I know I'm not there yet."

Isaac walked over to where Ethan was lying on a cot. "You've had six weeks of treatment, Ethan. And while we've seen a lot of progress, it's reasonable to think you'll need more time before you can handle the weight and physical demands of being a firefighter. That doesn't mean you won't get there. It only means you're going to need a little more time to strengthen your core and prepare for going back to work. We'll transition you to physical training to help you get ready."

"But you do think I will be able to do it eventually?" Ethan needed confirmation.

"The X-ray you had last week came back with good results. The surgery was successful. Isaac thinks you're ready to go back to work in another week or so. We'll start you off with light duty for a couple of months, but you'll be back at the station. That is what you want, right?"

"Yeah, I've really missed it," Ethan answered.

"After maybe eight weeks, you'll probably have to take a physical test to see if you can handle that aspect before you're cleared for full duty. It's one step at a time, Ethan. You'll get there."

"For the first time since the accident, I actually believe I'll be back on the truck. That's a good thing."

"What about your café?" Keira asked.

"I hope to do both," Ethan told her. "I really enjoy working at the café, as well, and of course, I want it to be successful. If it's too much for me to manage the café and continue to run shifts, I may look into shifting to more of a volunteer position with the fire department. And I may have to hire another cook for the café once Isa takes on more hours at the hospital. I'm just not sure yet."

Once his heat and stem treatment ended, Ethan grabbed his duffel bag and headed out the door. He stopped by the fire station to discuss his options with the chief now that his X-rays had come back positive and his therapy was soon ending. After meeting with the chief and setting a date for returning to the station on light duty, Ethan sat down to have lunch with the guys.

He had a plan, and he needed their help.

Isa stretched and then downed half a bottle of water before turning her attention back to the club sandwich she needed to create. The Second Chance Café's kitchen felt like her home away from home now. She finished plating the sandwich, checked on the soup of the day—French onion—pulled another meat loaf from one of the ovens and then tossed the Asian chicken salad with sesame dressing.

She tried not to feel sad about the fact that Ethan was returning to the café.

In all honesty, she was thrilled Ethan was doing so much better. She just wasn't sure she wanted to leave the café.

"The cake's ready, right, Isa?" Mark asked.

"It's in the cooler, but we should go ahead and set it out," Isa told him. Isa had planned a surprise "Welcome back, Ethan!" party for after closing. Company 51 had promised to come over, barring no emergency calls, of course. Ethan was supposedly picking Isa up for dinner and a movie, but instead they would celebrate his good news regarding his recovery.

The minute Mark flipped the Open sign to Closed, Isa's parents walked through the door, followed soon by Mandy and Leo and Maggie and José. The waitresses, Jenny and Kelly, wasted no time in bringing in balloons and hanging a banner they'd made. Isa brought out the cake.

Company 51 barreled into the café and the noise level skyrocketed. Isa kept an eye on the street, watching for Ethan's truck.

"He's here, you guys! Quiet down!" she yelled out. The room hushed, but as Ethan walked through the door, a loud rousing chorus of "Welcome back, Ethan!" filled the dining room. Ethan paused, placing his hand over his heart as though in shock, a wide smile on his face.

Isa served cake while Ethan made the rounds, saying hello to everyone. She looked out at the dining room filled with people, noise and laughter.

Family, friends, good food—there's something special about this café. I'm going to miss it so much.

"It's a lovely café, Isabella."

Isa looked at the table behind her, where her father sat smiling.

"Thanks, Dad. I mean, it's not mine, you know."

"I know," he said.

She grabbed the coffeepot and refilled her father's cup, then sat down next to him.

"You're looking well, Dad. It's amazing how far you've come since the surgery."

"I'm so thankful to God," he said.

"Me too," Isa whispered.

Her father tasted the cake in front of him.

"Did you make this?" he asked, and she nodded.

"I made an almond vanilla filling. I think it goes well with the buttercream frosting. You made something similar for mom's birthday several years ago." She waited for her father's assessment.

"It's very good, Isabella. I like it. So you did learn a thing or two in my kitchen, eh?" he said with a chuckle.

Isa grinned. "I suppose I did."

"How do you like running a kitchen?" her father asked.

"I'm a little embarrassed to say I'm loving it when I've given you and Leo so much grief over the years."

Her father chuckled. "It's all about finding your place, Isa, finding where *you* belong. What about nursing?" he asked gently, lowering his voice.

Isa sighed and looked at Ethan across the room. "I'm ready for a change, Dad. Admitting that sort of scares me. But I'm ready for a break from nursing."

"I heard Ethan's looking for a permanent cook," her father said.

Isa shook her head with a sad smile. "He hasn't asked me."

Her father didn't answer for a moment. "Maybe it's time you asked him."

Isa watched Ethan laugh loudly over by the firefighters. He caught her gaze across the room and winked at her.

"I think he's the one, Dad. I can picture my life with Ethan."

Her father nodded. "Then it's time to say yes, Isabella. It would be my privilege to walk you down the aisle."

Isa's eyes welled with tears. The fact that her dad *could* walk her down the aisle was an idea she'd given up on.

"He hasn't asked me, Dad. But if he does, I will take you up on that."

Her father leaned over and kissed the side of her head.

The sound of a loud siren across the street caused every firefighter in the room to jump to his feet. Emergency time. The guys filed outside quickly. Isa looked for Ethan but he must have walked outside with the guys.

"Isabella Romano!"

She froze in place at the sound of her name being yelled through a loudspeaker. She rushed outside with her family right behind her. Ethan stood in front of the Company 51 fire truck, with the guys of Company 51 flanking him.

"What's going on?" Isa asked, bewildered.

Ethan raised the loudspeaker microphone to his lips.

"I'm asking you to marry me." The words echoed through the parking lots of the café and the fire department.

Isa froze. Every eye was on her. Her jaw dropped and she covered her mouth with her hands.

"Well?" Ethan shouted with a grin. "Will you marry me?"

Isa lowered her hands, her smile widening and her whole body trembling. "Yes."

Every firefighter yelled in unison, "What was that?"

Isa laughed. "Yes!" she yelled. Cheers erupted and Isa cried.

Abundant life, Father. Thank You.

* * *

Ethan dropped the microphone and ran to where Isa stood. He cupped her face in his hands and sealed their moment with a kiss. Isa's family and the guys of Company 51 applauded.

Looking down at Isa and hearing the exuberant shouts of their family and friends surrounding them in front of the Second Chance Café, Ethan's heart filled. An unfamiliar sense of family came over him. He welcomed the sensation.

"So I was wondering," Isa began. "I heard you're looking for a permanent cook for the café."

Ethan's eyes widened. "Are you interested?"

"I might be. We need to talk salary, though. I want a raise."

Ethan laughed. He had a feeling that life with Isa would be one filled with more joy than he could ever have imagined.

"What's mine is yours, Isabella Romano," Ethan said before leaning down for another kiss.

* * * * *

REQUEST YOUR FREE BOOKS!

2 FREE INSPIRATIONAL NOVELS
PLUS 2
FREE
MYSTERY GIFTS

Love Inspired

YES! Please send me 2 FREE Love Inspired® novels and my 2 FREE mystery gifts (gifts are worth about $10). After receiving them, if I don't wish to receive any more books, I can return the shipping statement marked "cancel." If I don't cancel, I will receive 6 brand-new novels every month and be billed just $4.74 per book in the U.S. or $5.24 per book in Canada. That's a savings of at least 21% off the cover price. It's quite a bargain! Shipping and handling is just 50¢ per book in the U.S. and 75¢ per book in Canada.* I understand that accepting the 2 free books and gifts places me under no obligation to buy anything. I can always return a shipment and cancel at any time. Even if I never buy another book, the two free books and gifts are mine to keep forever.

105/305 IDN F49N

Name	(PLEASE PRINT)
Address	Apt. #
City	State/Prov.	Zip/Postal Code

Signature (if under 18, a parent or guardian must sign)

Mail to the **Harlequin® Reader Service:**
IN U.S.A.: P.O. Box 1867, Buffalo, NY 14240-1867
IN CANADA: P.O. Box 609, Fort Erie, Ontario L2A 5X3

**Are you a subscriber to Love Inspired books
and want to receive the larger-print edition?
Call 1-800-873-8635 or visit www.ReaderService.com.**

* Terms and prices subject to change without notice. Prices do not include applicable taxes. Sales tax applicable in N.Y. Canadian residents will be charged applicable taxes. Offer not valid in Quebec. This offer is limited to one order per household. Not valid for current subscribers to Love Inspired books. All orders subject to credit approval. Credit or debit balances in a customer's account(s) may be offset by any other outstanding balance owed by or to the customer. Please allow 4 to 6 weeks for delivery. Offer available while quantities last.

Your Privacy—The Harlequin® Reader Service is committed to protecting your privacy. Our Privacy Policy is available online at www.ReaderService.com or upon request from the Harlequin Reader Service.
We make a portion of our mailing list available to reputable third parties that offer products we believe may interest you. If you prefer that we not exchange your name with third parties, or if you wish to clarify or modify your communication preferences, please visit us at www.ReaderService.com/consumerschoice or write to us at Harlequin Reader Service Preference Service, P.O. Box 9062, Buffalo, NY 14269. Include your complete name and address.

LIDIR13R

REQUEST YOUR FREE BOOKS!

2 FREE INSPIRATIONAL NOVELS
PLUS 2
FREE
MYSTERY GIFTS

Love Inspired

HISTORICAL
INSPIRATIONAL HISTORICAL ROMANCE

YES! Please send me 2 FREE Love Inspired® Historical novels and my 2 FREE mystery gifts (gifts are worth about $10). After receiving them, if I don't wish to receive any more books, I can return the shipping statement marked "cancel." If I don't cancel, I will receive 4 brand-new novels every month and be billed just $4.74 per book in the U.S. or $5.24 per book in Canada. That's a savings of at least 21% off the cover price. It's quite a bargain! Shipping and handling is just 50¢ per book in the U.S. and 75¢ per book in Canada.* I understand that accepting the 2 free books and gifts places me under no obligation to buy anything. I can always return a shipment and cancel at any time. Even if I never buy another book, the two free books and gifts are mine to keep forever.

102/302 IDN F5CY

Name _____ (PLEASE PRINT) _____

Address _____ Apt. # _____

City _____ State/Prov. _____ Zip/Postal Code _____

Signature (if under 18, a parent or guardian must sign)

Mail to the Harlequin® Reader Service:
IN U.S.A.: P.O. Box 1867, Buffalo, NY 14240-1867
IN CANADA: P.O. Box 609, Fort Erie, Ontario L2A 5X3

Want to try two free books from another series?
Call 1-800-873-8635 or visit www.ReaderService.com.

* Terms and prices subject to change without notice. Prices do not include applicable taxes. Sales tax applicable in N.Y. Canadian residents will be charged applicable taxes. Offer not valid in Quebec. This offer is limited to one order per household. Not valid for current subscribers to Love Inspired Historical books. All orders subject to credit approval. Credit or debit balances in a customer's account(s) may be offset by any other outstanding balance owed by or to the customer. Please allow 4 to 6 weeks for delivery. Offer available while quantities last.

Your Privacy—The Harlequin® Reader Service is committed to protecting your privacy. Our Privacy Policy is available online at www.ReaderService.com or upon request from the Harlequin Reader Service.

We make a portion of our mailing list available to reputable third parties that offer products we believe may interest you. If you prefer that we not exchange your name with third parties, or if you wish to clarify or modify your communication preferences, please visit us at www.ReaderService.com/consumerschoice or write to us at Harlequin Reader Service Preference Service, P.O. Box 9062, Buffalo, NY 14269. Include your complete name and address.

LIHDIR13R

REQUEST YOUR FREE BOOKS!
2 FREE WHOLESOME ROMANCE NOVELS
IN LARGER PRINT
PLUS 2
FREE
MYSTERY GIFTS

✹✹✹✹✹✹✹✹✹✹✹✹✹✹✹✹✹✹✹✹✹✹✹✹

HEARTWARMING™

✹✹✹✹✹✹✹✹✹✹✹✹✹✹✹✹✹✹✹✹✹✹✹✹

Wholesome, tender romances

YES! Please send me 2 FREE Harlequin® Heartwarming Larger-Print novels and my 2 FREE mystery gifts (gifts worth about $10). After receiving them, if I don't wish to receive any more books, I can return the shipping statement marked "cancel." If I don't cancel, I will receive 4 brand-new larger-print novels every month and be billed just $4.99 per book in the U.S. or $5.74 per book in Canada. That's a savings of at least 23% off the cover price. It's quite a bargain! Shipping and handling is just 50¢ per book in the U.S. and 75¢ per book in Canada.* I understand that accepting the 2 free books and gifts places me under no obligation to buy anything. I can always return a shipment and cancel at any time. Even if I never buy another book, the two free books and gifts are mine to keep forever.

161/361 IDN F47N

Name _____ (PLEASE PRINT)

Address _____ Apt. #

City _____ State/Prov. _____ Zip/Postal Code

Signature (if under 18, a parent or guardian must sign)

Mail to the **Harlequin® Reader Service:**
IN U.S.A.: P.O. Box 1867, Buffalo, NY 14240-1867
IN CANADA: P.O. Box 609, Fort Erie, Ontario L2A 5X3

* Terms and prices subject to change without notice. Prices do not include applicable taxes. Sales tax applicable in N.Y. Canadian residents will be charged applicable taxes. Offer not valid in Quebec. This offer is limited to one order per household. Not valid for current subscribers to Harlequin Heartwarming larger-print books. All orders subject to credit approval. Credit or debit balances in a customer's account(s) may be offset by any other outstanding balance owed by or to the customer. Please allow 4 to 6 weeks for delivery. Offer available while quantities last.

Your Privacy—The Harlequin® Reader Service is committed to protecting your privacy. Our Privacy Policy is available online at www.ReaderService.com or upon request from the Harlequin Reader Service.

We make a portion of our mailing list available to reputable third parties that offer products we believe may interest you. If you prefer that we not exchange your name with third parties, or if you wish to clarify or modify your communication preferences, please visit us at www.ReaderService.com/consumerchoice or write to us at Harlequin Reader Service Preference Service, P.O. Box 9062, Buffalo, NY 14269. Include your complete name and address.

HWDIR13R

ReaderService.com

Manage your account online!
- Review your order history
- Manage your payments
- Update your address